THE NORTHERN COUNTIES COLLECTION

An anthology of poetry and short stories

Edited by Tim Saunders

Tim Saunders Publications

Copyright © 2022 Contributors

All rights reserved

No part of this book may be reproduced, or stored in a retrieval system, or transmitted in any form or by any means, electronic, mechanical, photocopying, recording, or otherwise, without express written permission of the publisher.

Cover design: Breaking Light - Skiddaw, 8 x 10", Patricia Haskey, patriciahaskey.co.uk

*This book celebrates the northern counties
of England: Lancashire, Yorkshire,
Durham and Northumberland.*

In the early morning the mill girls clumping down the cobbled street, all in clogs, making a curiously formidable sound, like an army hurrying into battle. I suppose this is the typical sound of Lancashire.

GEORGE ORWELL

CONTENTS

Title Page
Copyright
Dedication
Epigraph
LANCASHIRE   1
Foreword   2
POETRY   6
August 2018   7
The Fells   8
Clitheroe Knows Cheese   10
Mother's cooking   12
Happy Holiday   14
Yarrow Valley Country Park, Chorley   16
A badger named Richard and The Calf's Head   18
Brennand valley   21
Bull Spectators   23
Creativity Limit   24

Fred Dibnah's first chimney	25
Life's furrows	26
Hedge-laying stanzas	27
No Canal	28
Ridding Hey farm datestone to headstone	30
Shortest Night	32
Stone Metal Word	33
White Meteorites	34
Winda shoppin'	35
Lancashire Local fresh and homegrown	37
SHORT STORY	38
Recalling Peterloo	39
YORKSHIRE	44
Foreword	45
POETRY	47
The Song of Three Cross Wives	48
Haiku 1	49
Haiku 2	50
A Biscuit or two	51
Ode to the great	53
Speed Awareness Course, Huddersfield	55
SHORT STORIES	57
The gift horse	58
The man who broke the bank at Monte Carlo!	63

At the Harrogate Royal Pump Room	68
The Beach Hut	72
The End of the Line	74
The Little Pondering Preachathon	78
The Rock	83
Bob's Jubilee	87
Clara & Agatha's	92
DURHAM	97
Foreword	98
POETRY	99
Durham Castle	100
House	101
Freddie Williams's pigeons	104
Weardale Safari	106
Here's one I made	107
Return of the Lapwing	108
Remember the Miners	110
Tunstall Reservoir	112
Stanhope Bridge	113
Autumn light	114
Ordinary People	115
The Shoreline	119
A silver thread	121
Boudy	123

SHORT STORY	126
The Witness for the Prosecution	127
NORTHUMBERLAND	130
Foreword	131
POETRY	133
Hadrian's Wall…and beyond!	134
North East Bound	136
Lindisfarne	138
Tank Traps, Alnmouth	139
cobden burn cleugh	140
Dusk at Cheviot Hills	141
on hangman's hill	142
SHORT STORIES	144
Sanctuary	145
Freedom from shame	150
Northumberland Road	154
Tim Saunders Publications	159

LANCASHIRE

FOREWORD

Lancashire's diversity of people, towns, industry, rolling landscape and habitat always impresses me, even though I have lived here all but two of my almost sixty years. I could never claim to have experienced everything. Being a dairy farmer in Clitheroe for thirty-three years, instilled a deep appreciation of all the flora and fauna and the environs we all share. Moving on to the delivery logistics for an international company and subsequently doing over seven hundred miles every week in and around the county as a driving instructor for eight years made me appreciate Lancashire's wider beauty more. Vistas can be appreciated from many of our towns, the country lanes and picturesque villages all have a connected practical feel and still retain the fabric of their roots.

The flat moss land of the Fylde side peaked with Blackpool's heights and Morecambe's bay expanses gives way inland to the contrasting Bowland hills and fells, which hide one of my favourites, the Brennand valley. The bleakness of 'the trough' (Trough of Bowland) is equalled across the open treeless expanse of Pendle with its almost mountain deep cloughs. The panoramic splendour of Pendle's big end has to be experienced. On clear days the sea glints thirty miles west and the peaks of Yorkshire smile in the sun, north, with the contrasting more built environs of the Calder valley to the south peaked with the Rossendale fells. On less splendid days, moody windswept Pendle can hide in curtains of mizzle.

Rivers and their environs are also one of my loves and inspirations, even the industrial Calder can inspire. For me the river Ribble or Bellisima as the Romans probably named it has everything, coming down through Bolton by Bowland, past the otters cave and Pudsey's leap from its Yorkshire source, joined by the wild Hodder, it wends down to suckle the Irish sea at St Annes. Water always sustains bird and insect life, several nature reserves in and around the county, even in old quarries and gravel pits all add to the landscape quilt.

The combination of nature and man's interactions can almost be breathed in places. Scars on the landscape can be read, in the built environs too. Details often missed by most people are significant, usually more so for the past, but can have implications for the future, hopefully good. The Victorian and sometimes older architecture of various towns and villages is very impressive. With my qualifications in drystone walling and building abilities in traditional lime, I can really appreciate the craftsmanship and design.

Lancashire folks' enterprise, ingenuity and hardworking nature are greatly important to both past and present. We can proudly claim to be the cradle of the industrial revolution and the very first motorway. Today, many mills and chimneys have gone, some are re-used and a couple are heritage museums with the original steam engines to see. One now boasts the longest bar in the United Kingdom with the dormant Elisabeth engine a seriously unique spectacle, with a brewery in the same building. One legacy of the mill owners is their personal mansions and the contrasting terraced rows of houses built for many workers. These are still dominant in various places, some were only two room, one up one down properties.

Lancastrians are generally well-known as being friendly and hospitable types. Although if you ever saw the hilarious Renault Megane advert filmed in the village of Gisburn, you would say it was well hidden. Farmers with very dry humour and an enthusiastic Frenchman was a guarantee of contrasting mentality and humour. Still retaining much of its original charm and history there for all to see and not over-developed, wherever you are in Lancashire, rural vistas can soon encompass your every sense, without being touristy.

The impressive poems and short stories on the following pages reflect the outstanding beauty and diversity of Lancashire, the people and their language, all of whom write differently. Hopefully you find Lancashire's writers fresh and inspirational, maybe sufficiently so to pause and wonder, before penning some wonderful words of your own.

Andrew Collinson

POETRY

AUGUST 2018

It rained and rained and rained again,
the average fall was well maintained,
and when the tracks were simply bogs,
it started raining cats and dogs.
After a drought of half an hour,
we had a most refreshing shower,
and then the most curious thing of all,
a gentle rain began to fall.
Next day also was fairly dry,
save for a deluge from the sky,
which wetted us all to the skin
and after that, the rain set in.

Pete Etheridge

THE FELLS

Today their mood is peaceful, as
I walk the lonely fells,
however, be not deceived, for those floating
clouds would seek to envelop you and
hide you from the world outside,
as many a story tells.
Although the light is bright, as if the
sun is trying to find its way,
a soft breeze plays with my hair, and
raindrops strike my face,
bringing me to my senses and making me
aware of the beauty of this place.
The beauty of these dark, burnt heather slopes,
contrasting with the bracken, patched
with bilberry and fresh green heather.
The haunting cry of the curlew as it calls to
its chicks, beware, the merlin fleet of
feather.
The bleat of a woolly lamb can be heard
through the mist as it calls to another, then
bounds stiff-legged into view going on bended
knee to the black faced Swaledale ewe,
it's mother.
High in the sky the harrier glides with up-
stretched wings, eyes seeking to pierce the
mist where his mate sits on eggs below.
His enemies, two-legged and four- who, like

the ewe, walk the moor, not in peace but
bent on destruction.
Those who would walk the fells this day, are
foolish indeed to stray from the lonely path.
For when the clouds are low, clutching all to
their wet embrace, nature has only to
hide its track, then peat hag, bog or heather
sprig can throw a traveller on his back.
The fells then take on a different hue, of black
instead of blue, of horror, fear and hate.
For the man who travels unprepared
will surely meet his fate.

Pete Etheridge

Pete was employed by the RSPB as a Species Protection Officer in the Forest of Bowland. This meant spending long hours finding and keeping observation on birds of prey, in particular, the hen harrier.

CLITHEROE KNOWS CHEESE

for David Earith, The Cheese Stall, Clitheroe Market

Clitheroe's famed as the market for cheese –
knows how to trade 'em
promote and display 'em.
Can't fail with names like these:
Bob's Knobs cheese (Leagrams Organic)
waxed in red and partly in green,
looks, like Mount Etna, extremely volcanic
and it sells for its name alone.
Kick Ass cheese can't help but please
by bringing a tear to the eye.
Lancashire Black Bomb, how's yer father
I ask yer, what's not to like?
Dewlay, Greenfields, Butler's, Kirkham's
wonderful cheese-making talents!
Then there's crumbly Sandhams,
Nicky Nook – one of the grand 'uns,
Trotter Hill Tasty, Goosnargh Goats cheese
Grandma Singletons, Lancashire Ewes.
Not to be hasty, but, goodness! Oh please!
Try the lot. What have you got to lose?

Philip Burton

Philip Burton is a family man, born in Fife,

raised in Thanet, and has been a hippie, a labourer, a professional student, and a Lancashire headteacher. In 2019, Philip concurrently held three poetry competition first prizes: the Jack Clemo, the Sandwich (Kent) Poet of the Year, and the Barn Owl Trust. In 2021 he won the East Riding Poetry competition. His poetry books include: The Raven's Diary, Couples, His Usual Theft, Gaia Warnings and The Life Dyslexic.

MOTHER'S COOKING

It wasn't the tripe and onions
the steamy black puddings
or Lancashire hot pot
made from the scrag end of lamb
that I missed when I left home
but mother's pies filled with rhubarb
picked fresh from the garden
or gooseberries when they were in season
and raspberries, blackberries, bilberries
lemon tarts heaped with meringue cones
butterfly buns topped with whipped cream
and dollops of raspberry jam
custard slices smothered in icing,
the custard oozing out when you bit into them
Eccles cakes jam-packed with currants
drop scones and hot-crossed buns at Easter
lemon curd, strawberry jam and marmalade
- all of it homemade.

Jennifer Palmer

Jennifer is a member of Clitheroe Writing group, which belongs to NAWG. She lives in rural Lancashire where she was born. Jennifer spent her working life teaching English in London and abroad. She writes poetry, short stories and local history, inspired by the Pendle area where she lives. Jennifer has published two memoirs, a book of short stories, a book of poems and two family history books, the latest is Witches, Quakers and Nonconformists.

HAPPY HOLIDAY

I can't wait to have my holiday,
I've got my coat and hat
I haven't packed the sun cream,
I'm sure I won't need that
I'm off to stay at Blackpool, I've
saved all through the year
it was sunny when I set off, but will
be raining soon, I fear.
I fell in love with Blackpool at
the tender age of three
now it seems a different place at
the age of seventy-three.
I bought a bucket and a spade and
began to build a castle
then the tide came round me, oh
bother, what a hassle.
I paddled through the water getting
my new trainers wet
and then I lost my false teeth, now
I'd need a brand new set
but I still loved dear old Blackpool,
as I squelched along the mile
and watching kids eat candyfloss,
I couldn't help but smile.
I bought a bag of fish and chips,
full of grease and fat
and then it started raining, where

was my plastic hat?
I went back to my little room, feeling
drenched and all alone.
I really thought that it was time, to
have a right good moan.
I thought I'd meet a partner, a toyboy,
or some such thing
But I was disappointed, when,
no one would have a fling
I said goodbye to Blackpool,
I'd had a week of untold joy
it would take all year to save again,
I couldn't wait, oh boy.

Elizabeth Naisbitt

Elizabeth lives in Burnley. Many years ago she was involved with Pendle Writers and has had poems and short stories published. She has now discovered Burnley Writers' Circle which keeps her inspired.

YARROW VALLEY COUNTRY PARK, CHORLEY

through the seasons

Snowdrops timidly whisper of a new year filled with hope. Their small, fragile flowers gently give way to randomly scattered wild daffodils lifting their sunshine faces to the sky heralding in a time of new life and rebirth. The mist rises mysteriously from the lake as swans emerge coalescing into phantom forms with tiny cygnets drifting in their wake. The seamless transition from tremulous spring into heavily scented hazy days of summer sees a kaleidoscope of flowers bursting into life. The kingfisher reflects the azure blue of sun-kissed skies as migratory birds fly alongside resident native species. A time to linger and marvel at sunshine fields of gold set in cathedral boughs of emerald green. And as the evening sun sets on lazy summer days, autumn's fiery splendour licks the flame of evening light, as oak, ash and birch claw the sky with strength and power. Reflected in the waters' depths they stand, tall and proud in their evening gowns of browns, dark greens

and gold lighting up the darkening sky.
Steel grey skies give way to winter's icy touch
as snow-flakes drift across the frozen waters
to rest on sleepy barren boughs laden with
snow. The peace is all encompassing with the
damp smell of earth, wood and pine creating
a deep inner warmth as seagulls circle high
above catching thermals in flight.
And so the months and years turn from winter's
nurturing rest to spring's tender beginnings,
summer's lazy days and autumn's golden glory
to come full circle in the creation of life.

Eleanor Mary Nelson

As a child Eleanor drifted in her own fantasy world of faeries, mystery and magic, to the annoyance of her teachers. Hobbies have been varied: multi-cultural dancing, ballet, writing, recording music, artistic film production, sculpting and writing poetry. Eleanor is writing a fantasy trilogy called Mutant World. She loved being a social worker. Extensive travel opened her eyes to world economic and social problems. She has a deep and abiding love of nature and the earth.

A BADGER NAMED RICHARD AND THE CALF'S HEAD

Tourist Bishop Polcocke on visiting Clitheroe from Ireland in 1750 noted, "The small town's business of lime and mill work made them very thirsty, giving a habit of drinking." He got the gist… Read as part of the 2018 Heritage Weekend, outside what was the Calf's Head.

White bones under blackthorn's creamy stars
a brock's* boney remains were collected
the year we took the Badgers Starr pasture
aside the ancient Pimlico to Worston track
Calf's Head, a load on his back.
Badgers Starr, means what?
After thirty years historic tracking
grey became black and white.
Badgers Starr means what?
An odd field name coincidence, it's not.
Longhorn or shorthorn
the Calf's Head's not there
last thatch of Clitheroe's market square
kept Badgers dry, behind bars
in the Vic's black and white fat face location.
Alexander & Bowden quilled every

field, owner and tenant
Their 1822 survey revealed a
black and white match.
The Badgers Starr was Great Starr
pasture, owner Richard Badger
under thatch, the Calf's Head publican is dead
but his name-sake's old bones are in
a shoebox, under my bed.

Andrew Collinson

* badger. The Ribble valley has quite a few place names with brock in and some surnames do, too. Brockholes, Brockholes brow and Brocklehurst to name but a few.

Notes

Andrew writes: "The coincidence of finding the old badger's skeleton, in our new field when I was 12, was remarkable. Our neighbour Leo Begley had the field before us and told us it was called Badgers Starr. After much research I found it was originally Great Starr, owned by Richard Badger, hence Badgers Starr... landlord of the Calf's Head, not in Worston as today, but the Market Square, Clitheroe. The skeleton, which I still have was layed out under the hedge at the side of the ancient track to Worston, which ran from Pimlico, before the construction of Chatburn new road past Bellman in 1826. The Badger clan ran the Calf's Head in Worston for about 100 years."

TIM SAUNDERS

BRENNAND VALLEY

A Peregrine hawks the valley
pinprick high above the crag
hunting pigeon, rapid stooping brag.
Dippers inhabit the brook
bobbing, shouting and diving for grub.
Beefers graze, high under the fell wall
mineral licks in a tub.

Rushy fields too steep to mow
altitude boundary for grass to grow
broken hills, water washed weathered
moss peat grass and stone, rest heathered
graded scree slopes steep broken stones,
shattered rocks, brown bracken frills
sharp edged blocky boulders, bold treeless hills.

Curvy green and white Dalmations,
rabbit and sheep nibbled valley floor,
tortured water scribbled
trees hide in gullies sheltered, barely seen, few
dark fells divided, raggy trees, autumn hue
mellow shades, greens browns and dun
natures grounded patchwork run.

Elevated unseen isolation, worship place of old
tight between hill ends, peaty and bald
Brennand Tarn, mysterious black and deep

Stone Age axe head, Swaledale sheep
babbling brook, lost lamb bleat.

Andrew Collinson

BULL SPECTATORS

There were two
stood by the yard gate
one winter morning.
We talked for a while and cracked a smile
about Iggy, our placid Blonde d'Aquitaine bull
sniffing and turning his nose ring up
checking his 60 cow harem.
Solid, double muscled, over a ton
easy going, but needed respect
thin skinned, long bodied and lish
un-staved muscles in his barrelled neck.
I approached him
reassured him, rubbed his back
pulled the skin on his ribs
a snorty head-swing warned me off.
Both spectators
Paul senior and Paul junior
still mention Iggy and how we met.

Andrew Collinson

CREATIVITY LIMIT

Straight forward basic life
complicated by living
insignificant activities
essential essentials, essentially
I'll live my way, I'll die one day.
Sanity is the crazy
restraining eccentricity
living in real time eyes
the buffers of real skies
the blinkered genius fries
reigned creation, monotony motivation.
Everyday resignation, imagination stifle
future dreams, behind the everyday.
Shoot me
use my rifle.

Andrew Collinson

FRED DIBNAH'S FIRST CHIMNEY

Bolton's Albert Street roof-line wer re-med
aged 16 is stack wer' drawn an' built
Victorian style, reet fanci
Wen mutha Betsy cem ome, it wer' pointin tut sky
an Accrington Nori brick pain in't eye - thowt she.
Now protected, as heritage shud be.
Folks from a far stare n' gawp, tha see
at fost chimney Fred dezined n' med
an- it still sticks sky-wud
like a brick balustrade, ower - 'ed.

Andrew Collinson

LIFE'S FURROWS

Steadily folded parallel rutted habits
our corrugated furrows; conceal, dig, reveal
sand silt 'n clay disturbed
our biography profile, polishes the
mouldboards[1] of time.
Rack of eye[2] steers, re-invents
stony memories scar mental Ransome[3]
sand silt 'n clay re-worked
a cycle of existence - blacks life's field.
Relentless on we plough, years turn over
sand silt 'n clay, cultivates vigour
evocative friable tilth[4], buries life's debris
left behind and reused, earthy
nutrition for root-growing thought.

Andrew Collinson

1. *mouldboard* curved part of a plough which lifts and turns the soil over
2. *Rack of eye* (dialect) meaning visual judgement
3. *Ransome* famous make of plough
4. *friable tilth* well cultivated soft crumbly seed bed

HEDGE-LAYING STANZAS

Untrimmed moribund pages prevail
idioms smothered in subjects of wood
overgrown phrases branch tangled
thorny alliteration, bull-skin glove wrangled
commas, quicks and gatepost full-
stops punctuate.
Heavy Ash text and Elderberry
embellishments sawn dead.
Therapeutic clarity, laying poem or hedge
mental slasher, axes, pen, and
snippers verbiage dredge.
Live horizontals and deadwood edited out.
Axed compositions survive on tenuous sapwood
spikey lines cleaved at heels point,
timber italics lean
a rhythm of usable trees, tied by
snipped stumpy words
pricking-post margins, restrain stanzas with a nail
un-battered by public flail.

Andrew Collinson

NO CANAL

The nearest we ever had, an 800
yard hand-dug feat
Lowmoor cut, the big mill leat.
Clitheroe had no E on the end
as 1776 Yorkshire-Lancashire canal was planned
Bradford mill owners need, lime on demand.

They argued round a Burnley
table the route to adopt
Barlick via Pimlico to Preston was dropped.
Liverpool merchants had more
brass, the port more draw
still the northern branch by Altham
plugged in Clitheroe.

Aqueduct over the Calder, an airborne
stab near Whalley Nab
ambitious plan of intended navigable canal
but locally it fell, apathy of
landowners, slow death knell.
Twenty years later twice proposed, 24 years on
when town was some 600 houses strong.

Advantages Baines did predict of
"soon connection to the navigation
to enrich this district".

But investors feared as turnpikes appeared
priority for lime changed to coal through time
1845 marked the coming of the iron road
so Leeds Liverpool Canal navies never
dug - any Clitheroe node.

Andrew Collinson

RIDDING HEY FARM DATESTONE TO HEADSTONE

Optimism chiselled Riddiough's bold
initials on Clitheroe's oldest habitation
rebuilt - ACR1683. Steadily black powder
brast* away Ridding Hey - forever.
Depleted in Chatburn old road
isolation, decades hobbled
on the narrow high alter, another
sacrificial farmstead.
Atop the now vacuous space a millennium
before wispy brown smoke rose.
Empty silence acknowledged the terminal boom.
One of four demolished, with thirty-
six generations traced
only rock and coin count in the irreversible
wake of pillage industry dust.
Good bedrock furnished fertile friable
soil for yeomen's show winners.
Insidious dynamite plough effects were
emphasized with tungsten teeth.
The final heavy harvest, an everlasting
infertile mono-crop of air.
Skylarks daren't descend the deepening hole.
Tewitts have no insects to feed

young, no horses to curse
Curlews have no fields to shrill, nest or probe
Sparrows have no piggin or grain to scavenge
Twitcher's watch disheartened pin-prick
seagulls fossick for non-existent food
four hundred feet down, on hard barren
terra or fluorescent water.
Gillet and Klondike conjoined
Bankfield quarries, now relay
medieval Hey's buckthorn boundaries,
tethered in ether.
Mario's online slider proves calcium
carbonate tilled the greenery.
Demand for the same starved flora and
fauna longevity, destroyed landscape
skyline and farm - datestone to headstone.
Random limestone walls, kitted
in lime sheltered farmer
come lime-burner William Briggs, was his
wit as dry? Would he see the irony?
Ever-subterranean demigod questing
more, his mercenary decedents
sacrificed Ridding Hey, alter kilns fired
raw building to white dust
his genes, old chair and clogs were fuel.

Andrew Collinson

*burst

SHORTEST NIGHT

Summer sunset shower, colours fade by the hour
earth warm and damp at dusk, nostrils
teased with evening musk
smells growy, with deep ocean sky, good
day tomorrow, pressure high
fleets of midges fly, swifts scream, last goodbye.
Seedling stars grow on the dark backdrop
mellow moon breaks the horizon,
few wispy clouds
brave moonlit dark, soft glow-
light, winched lofty, bright
earth warmly bathed in reflected light
a solitary fox barks across the valley.
Wandering monochrome cows quietly graze
everything shades of grey, gentle
warm wafts of drying hay.
Stars sink back and fade away, east
horizon promising day
temperature drop signals grassy dews
mist softly hangs, as day renews.

Andrew Collinson

STONE METAL WORD

Stone quarry
stone quarryman
stone worker
quarry worker
quarry labourer
stone mason
stone chisel
cold chisel
metal worker
whitesmith
silversmith
tinsmith
goldsmith
blacksmith
wordsmith;
black art
word art.

Andrew Collinson

WHITE METEORITES

Bitter wind
             near horizontal
l u m
 py
cold   rain.
Occasional
heavy snowflakes
        oblique
         white
         meteorites.
Thud silently
on snod ground
  icy drips
    hat
    to
    n
    e
    c
    k
seldom seen
  never
                found.

Andrew Collinson

WINDA SHOPPIN'

We olas did it as kids
mi sista, me n' mutha
fatha nare did
eh wer olas werkin.

Nobut three on us
browsin fer dreams
opin t' spot summat
famli cud aford.

Toys, grub, cloys
bobbin' i' shop door oles
outat cowd wind
just avin a sken.

Me fave wert gunsmith
gaupin' throu t' glass
unt bars, usin mi ans
like os blinkers.

So a cud see
allt luvly stuff thi ad.
Like that Bowie lock knife
n yon 4 10 gun, wi nare cud aford.
Any road, poin-tis
why's killin time fur nowt
cawd winda shoppin?

Folks naer shop fer windas.

Andrew Collinson

Born in 1964 and raised in north east Lancashire, Andrew was destined to have rural blood. Dairy farming for thirty-three years, a mile from where he attended Clitheroe Royal Grammar School, the scenic village of Sabden is now home. A Lancashire Wildlife Trust member, an agricultural engineer and former driving instructor he has three children and four grandsons. Landscapes, traumatic loss of the farm, nature, weather and man's destructive ability are among his diverse and observant writing inspirations. Andrew's work has been published in CWG and Poetry Society Stanza group anthologies and the last Pendle War Poetry publication of 2018.

LANCASHIRE LOCAL FRESH AND HOMEGROWN
a brief history of food in Lancashire

Moorland, meadow, mudflats and more
Celts fished trout, foraged in forests and seas
Lancashire local, fresh and home grown.
Romans left marks with cherry seeds sown
Danes farmed the land for rich butter and cheese
moorland, meadow, mudflats and more.
Norman cutlery and condiments set a refined tone
fine ales from peat water, for mead thank the bees
moorland, meadow, mudflats and more.
Muttony gluttony caused monks to groan
mill workers came home to spud pie and peas
Lancashire local fresh and homegrown.
Now modern Lancastrians order by phone
fusion food feasts inspired overseas
moorland, meadow, mudflats and more
Lancashire local fresh and homegrown

Rosemary Moore

SHORT STORY

RECALLING PETERLOO

By Jennifer Palmer

> Oldham
> August
> 1832

Dear William,

I hope this letter finds you alive and well. It is so long since I heard anything about you. It was a long time before I found out that you were one of the unfortunate souls deported to Botany Bay after the massacre in Peterloo. Many years have passed since that fateful day in 1819, when you bore the standard on behalf of us handweavers and spinners. What a cruel fate! I only hope your life has been tolerable.

You will recall just how hot that summer of 1819 was. It had followed many years of rain and crop failure. Times were hard for us handweavers and spinners. Our wages had kept falling and the price of bread had kept rising. Is it any wonder that we took it upon ourselves to travel to Manchester to listen to Orator Hunt* addressing the crowd in St Peter's Fields? If anyone could make the government listen, it was him.

Our cause was righteous enough. We were

after a fair wage for our long hours of work and representation in parliament. It wasn't much to ask. If we stood up for our rights, we thought, they would surely be granted. How wrong we were!

Our lives were very different. I did my weaving at home, aided by my wife and children. All I needed was a room and some candles. I could work all the hours of the night, if need be, whereas you spinners had to clock on and off. We earned less than you but our time was our own. Yet we handweavers had much in common with you spinners and we fought alongside each other for a common cause in our reform group.

As you know, I was the secretary of our group and so it was me who decided we should have our own flag to take to the demonstration. I got the idea for the slogan from one I had seen over in Saddleworth, which read 'Equal representation or death'. It had two hands clasping underneath, like they have on tombstones. That is why the authorities called it ungodly. But it was they who were the ungodly ones, the way they treated us, the way they treated you.

Workers all over Lancashire, in Middleton and Bolton, in Preston and Blackburn, were standing up for themselves. Who could blame them? Nothing will change of its own accord. How sorry I was that I couldn't go with you to carry the flag. If only I hadn't come down with that bout of flu. I had no doubt brought it upon myself by burning the candle at both ends. My wife forbade me to leave the house. She said it would be the death of me. It took me all that summer to shake off the sickness. And I have never been the same since.

But I don't wish to dwell on my own woes. Your fate has been far worse than mine. I heard from your wife that you were injured that day. When the yeomanry was let loose on the crowd, they lashed out at all and sundry. You were one of the unfortunate ones. Thank God you weren't killed. It was all to stop Orator Hunt from speaking and the crowd from listening. Your wife tells me she defended you at the assizes as best she could but it was all in vain. They were determined to punish you, come what may, to make an example of you.

You were not to blame. You were the one who held the flag but I was the one who made it. I would have told them so if I'd been there. To this day I regret that I wasn't. Who knows if they would have listened to such as me? By the time I had recovered from my illness, your trial was over and you'd been sent to God knows where. It was years before I found out your fate.

It is hard these days to make a living in Oldham. When once we weavers earned twenty or thirty shillings a week, we are now lucky to earn four or five. Some people have been forced into selling their furniture to get by. Others have even sold the clothes off their backs. But we have not stood idly by. Now we are demanding that we should be able to earn a decent living, without working all the hours God sends us, and for our children to go to school and have a say in their future.

The government has finally got round to bringing in changes. They are calling it The Representation of the People Act. It will mean that Manchester and other cities like it will have two Members of Parliament to represent them. The vote is to be extended to include people with households, which have a rental value of ten pounds a year or more. The fight must go on until every man and woman has the vote.

I cannot imagine what your life has been like since you were banished to the farthest reaches of the earth. We hear such terrible tales about life over there. But your day will soon come. What will you do when you are set free? Where will you go?

This year we have had a warm spring and the earth has been generous. There are now mushrooms springing up everywhere. The potatoes and turnips are multiplying in the fields and we are about to start gathering in the hay. There's even hope of a second crop. We have just enjoyed the best crop of gooseberries we've ever had and are looking forward to a bountiful harvest.

If this letter reaches you, and if you have the good fortune to make the arduous journey home, remember that you are always welcome in my house. I will have a jar of my own home-brewed ale ready and waiting.

Your sincere friend,

John

* Henry "Orator" Hunt (November 6, 1773 to February 13, 1835) was a British radical speaker who pioneered working-class radicalism. He was an important influence on the later Chartist movement and advocated parliamentary reform as well as the repeal of the Corn Laws.

Jennifer is a member of Clitheroe Writing group, which belongs to NAWG. She lives in rural Lancashire where she was born. Jennifer spent her working life teaching English in London and abroad. She writes poetry, short stories and local history, inspired by the Pendle area where she lives. Jennifer has published two memoirs, a book of short stories, a book of poems and two family history books, the latest is Witches, Quakers and Nonconformists.

YORKSHIRE

FOREWORD

I am honoured to be part of a book about the north, and I am especially pleased to write the introduction to the chapter on Yorkshire.

Yorkshire to me is my childhood home. It is my parents arguing over whether Yorkshire or Lancashire is better. (Of course, Yorkshire.) Yorkshire is summertime on my grandparent's farm - venturing out into the corn fields before retreating in defeat with my eyes and nose streaming from hayfever.

Growing up, I lived in a small village and dreamed of moving to a big city. I lived in some of the biggest cities in the world and dreamed of returning to Yorkshire. I am happy to be home with my parents, raising my children with a garden and clean air.

Yorkshire is many things - it is the Dales and the coast. It is the hustle and bustle of seaside resorts such as Whitby with its vampires and towering whalebones; it is the grit and determination of industrial behemoths such as Bradford and Leeds. It is old cities such as York and Ripon and spa towns like Harrogate. To me, Yorkshire is a special place, and the writing in this section shows our unique spirit.

Solvig Choi

POETRY

THE SONG OF THREE CROSS WIVES

comedy poem derived from the story of Shadrach, Meshach, and Abednego, short listed in the York Literature Festival Poetry Competition 2020

Turning up outside our houses
with no shoes and socks, no trousers,
nothing on! Three shameful strippers!
… Smelling like a crate of kippers.
Is there nothing that abashes
you three more-than-naked flashers
singed from head to toe, quite hairless?
How could you have been so careless?
"We were roasted in the furnace
and, although it didn't burn us,
all our clothes went up like tinder,
leaving not a single cinder."
Yet another likely story
made up in pursuit of glory!
We know you three ne'er-do-wellers,
all accomplished porky-tellers.
This is just to boost your ego,
Shadrach. Meshach? Abednego!

Neville Judson

HAIKU 1

Mountain tarn at dusk
rippled by a chilling wind
that blows but briefly.

Neville Judson

HAIKU 2

In total darkness
water dripping onto stone
makes distant voices.

Neville Judson

Neville Judson lives in rural north Yorkshire, not far from Harrogate. He grew up in south Derbyshire, where, he says, he had the good fortune to be taught by an enthusiastic and inspiring English teacher. He is well-known for his articles about caving and his scientific writing about uses of artificial intelligence in chemical research, published under the name, Philip Judson.

A BISCUIT OR TWO

I have just returned from a run
time to kick my feet back with a brew
surely I won't be harming my figure
if I have a biscuit or two.
I cannot help but snack
when the biscuit barrel is plain in sight
I always binge eat pretty much every day
and then I go to bed feeling guilty at night.
There is nothing wrong with a cheeky treat
a little biscuit on the sassy whim
I always tell myself not to feel guilty
because tomorrow I will be back in the gym!
They always say a little treat won't hurt
to taste that sweet sensation
but I can't do with minute helpings
I certainly can't eat in moderation!
When a fresh packet is out in sight
the biscuits are gone in a shot
because I cannot just eat the one
I have to eat the whole bloody lot!
Sometimes I do try and resist
and the healthy eating is going strong
but then the biscuits will be out at
work and I am tucking in
the diet didn't last very long!
As long as I keep up with my fitness
and I don't think of it as a taboo

there is nothing wrong with kicking back my feet
and having a biscuit or two!

Jamie Harry Scrutton

Jamie (33) is a Leeds based artist, specialising in performance poetry and animation.

ODE TO THE GREAT

Great people I have known
are no longer here
… a fact I bemoan.
The good die young, someone did say
I've known such people
who've guided me on the way.
I recall those who've lost life
from Max, first to pass
to Ali, best friend of my wife.
Those from a bygone era
consigned to the past
replaced by those inferior.
While cruel to cut life short
there must be a reason
their ship left the port.
Once on hand with advice
these friends and mentors
you remember, which is nice.
Treasured advice they gave
how to tackle life's challenges
their presence felt from't grave.
Dependable and strong
they continue to support
despite being gone so long.
It's heartening when feeling unsure
that valuable lessons were learnt
from those who went before.

They had my respect and admiration
always knowing what to do
and today they give inspiration.

TA Saunders

TA Saunders was born in Wakefield in April 1978 as it snowed. His poetry, written since childhood, has been published in numerous anthologies and some magazines. A collection of his work titled Poems for Today is widely available.

SPEED AWARENESS COURSE, HUDDERSFIELD

You could segment the mood with a butter knife –
not-my-fault downmouths, mardy shoulders,
fierce dunk action into blistering tea – burnt
fingers nothing on missing a day's pay for this
fatuous no-choice what's the point waste of hours.

Fretbraids twists his pen. Miss Yorkshire doodles
cube on cube while Stuffed Shirt gazes at the wall,
taps the Tag Heuer at intervals. The vicar spins
her claddagh – where the hell's
that genie got to now?
Two puff-chested firemen scan the room
for trouble, keen to get the bastards ticked
and off the list – stun 'em with stats and facts
and – listen up – for today's lesson we have
(drumroll please) some roadside
hardware and a DVD.

The twinkles from Miss Pink Cat's brooch cast
little trills of light along the melamine while
Ironman beats a tattoo with his fingers – rat ta taa
rat ta taa – keeps time with his inner marathon.

And nowhere, ladies and gents,
in forgodssakecalmdown.uk

and threemorepoints.britain
is there a greater sense of
we're all in this together.

Rose Egan

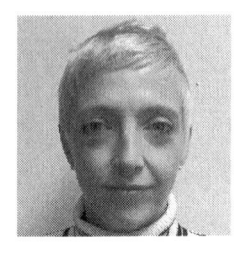

Rose lives in Ryde on the Isle of Wight and is a sub-editor, who has worked on media and financial magazines. In 2021 she finished her degree in English Literature and Creative Writing and is now reading a Masters in Poetry. "I write poems about what I see around me," says Rose, who has four children aged 15 to 21 and a beagle called Draco. She has lived in London, Hong Kong, Germany and Australia. "I'm always drawn back to Ryde," she reveals. "I can genuinely say that there's nowhere else I'd rather be." More of Rose's poetry features in The Isle of Wight Collection published by Tim Saunders Publications.

SHORT STORIES

THE GIFT HORSE

By Dan Boylan

MARCIA unlocked the front door and let herself in. She flicked the hall light on, pushed the door shut, picked up the mail and dropped the deadlock; she shrugged off her coat and turned up the central heating. Catching a glimpse of her face as she passed the hall mirror she gasped at her sudden drawn and haggard appearance.

"Better go and get yourself a glass of brandy, girl, it's been a long day."

A tortoiseshell cat strolled regally out of the sitting room, stretched, arched its back and gave a purr of recognition, which probably meant, "where's my dinner?"

"Hello, Monsieur Henri, sorry I've been away for so long, it took longer than expected but I've been rather busy. One five star serving of salmon delight coming up."

She pressed the on switch on the stereo and a mellow Johnny Mathis oozed seductively out of the speaker............chances are you think that I'm awfully good..........

The cat brushed against her leg as she placed the bowl of salmon delight on the kitchen floor. Marcia opened the fridge door and prepared a plateful of salad, cold ham and cheese and poured herself a glass of chilled Sauvignon blanc, laid it on a tray and carried it through to the dining room. Her eyes focused on the plate and she was about to start when her mobile phone jingled into life. She peered at the display screen, saw *mother* and tutted, audibly. She dithered momentarily, and then pressed OK.

"Hello mother," she said, without enthusiasm. She listened, without emotion and answered, "It went as well as you could expect a funeral to go. There was a small gathering, some of his old workmates and his son from up north was there. I went from the church to the crem, then back to the White Hart for tea and sandwiches and after half an hour made my excuses and left."

She listened again, then said, "Don't apologise, I wasn't expecting you to come mother, it's an awful long way and you'd only met Jim a couple of times."

The response took longer and the air heavy with her obvious impatience and irritation. "Thank you for the invitation mother but there's an awful lot to be done here. I have to wind up his affairs, sort the will, insurance, and change all the utility services into my name. It's going to take me weeks. I'll come up when everything is sorted and I've had a little break, probably in Florida. I'll call you in a few days to let you know how I'm doing. Look after yourself, bye-bye."

Marcia attacked the salad with gusto, took a

sip of wine and cleared her plate. Demis Roussos seeped alluringly from the speakers 'ever and ever and ever and ever you'll be the one' and she stopped in mid stride and did a pirouette and let out a deep chuckle.

The cat strolled across the faded Axminster as Marcia grinned, "Well, Monsieur Henri, what do you think? Have we pulled it off? If we have, then it's all been well worth the effort and inconvenience," she paused, "it was all part of the plan you know, I intended all this from the beginning." And she stared at him, her brow furrowed and an edge of guilt on her voice.

"I was desperate after Michael left, he left me with little money, nowhere to live and no means of support. I had nothing but the clothes I stood up in. Mother took me in but made it clear it was only a short-term measure. I had to find somewhere else, someone else and someone unattached, with their own home and savings; then as if by magic, mon petit chou, up pops old Jim, widowed, solvent and with a long list of medical conditions. What you might call a silver lining or the pot of gold at the end of the rainbow. I wooed him, charmed him and moved in with him all in two short weeks. His son and daughter didn't like it but it was me or them."

The cat purred and leapt onto her lap and snuggled down as if to listen to the monologue as Frank Sinatra crooned from the radio, 'after you've gone, there's no denying, after you've gone..........'

"Oh, thank you Mr Sinatra, thank you, how very appropriate."

The cat stirred and she stroked his back, "There, there, I didn't mean to frighten you." Then a pause and she became reflective again. "I made him very comfortable during his last few months mon chou, I cooked his favourite meals, let him smoke his pipe in the conservatory and made sure there was always a bottle of Famous Grouse in the drinks cabinet. I'll admit I didn't always make sure he took his heart tablets or trouble him to take some exercise, I never did bother to send him to the doctors in case they took his blood pressure, you understand."

The cat slept as Tom Jones pounded out, 'what's new pussycat?'

But she ignored the music and the sleeping moggy, driven no doubt by the urge to share her innermost secrets and perhaps her guilt and maybe even her good fortune. "His family thought I was a gold digger Henri, you know and completely overlooked the fact that I was looking after a tired and lonely old man, and I might say, a very grateful old man. After we married, he made me joint owner of the house, his bank accounts, his insurance policies and signed anything I put before him, especially when he'd had a dram or two."

Another generous measure of wine splashed into the glass. "His family will be waiting for the will to be read," she announced, "but by then, we'll be long gone mon ami, the house will be up for sale and we will have moved to a rather nice apartment near Pont Neuf. Oh, I do love Paris, and we shall soon be holidaying on the Riviera." Paul McCartney and co carouseled her with his old reminder that 'money can't buy you love'. "Perhaps not, Mr MacCartney," she agreed, "but it will buy you a lovely, fashionable apartment on tres chic, Rue Madeleine!"

She poured another top up as she reached for the mail, cast aside the junk and opted for the plain white envelope. She pealed it open and read aloud, 'Dear Mrs Harris, Please find attached a copy of Mr Harris's last will and testament, signed in my presence last week, three days before he died. You will see that all previous wills and all bank accounts and joint ownerships are thus superseded leaving his entire estate to his son and daughter'.
Sincerely, J.S. Morris, L.L.B Carter's Solicitors.

Her piercing screech terrified Monsieur Henri, who catapulted across the kitchen tiles, underneath the table and flung himself, headlong, through the cat flap.

THE MAN WHO BROKE THE BANK AT MONTE CARLO!

By Dan Boylan

THAT famous old music hall song about a man who made a fortune on the roulette tables at Monte Carlo has found its way into popular legend but is based on a true story.

The Victorians, like us, just loved a story of a working class man making a packet at the expense of the rich, affluent upper classes. One man did, and they loved it so much, they wrote a song about it.

He was not a 19th century dandy, nor a cardsharp or a slick, smooth con-man but a quiet, unassuming mill engineer with an intimate knowledge of spinning machines. Joseph Hobson Jagger was born in September 1830 in a weaving mill district of northern England.

In 1873 he went on holiday to the south of France and whilst there, would wander in to the Beaux Arts casino at Monte Carlo after dinner and watch the punters playing at the roulette wheels. He was fascinated by the new sporting technology and over the course of several days, developed a theory that the wheels at certain tables had a tendency to favour particular numbers. The engineer in him would not accept that the roulette wheels operated by chance and dropped the ball into one of thirty-six slots at random.

He employed six assistants and had them record the resulting numbers of each of the six roulette wheels during a twelve-hour period. Then, for a week, armed with pen, paper and mental arithmetic, he painstakingly computed the odds and slowly developed a system. He analysed his findings and discovered that five of the wheels consistently turned up a random series of numbers... whilst the sixth wheel showed a clear tendency to repeat three particular numbers.

As an engineer, he concluded that the wheel's central spindle had probably become slightly worn and the roulette wheel's balance had, in turn, become marginally tilted, allowing the ball to fall repeatedly into a certain section of the wheel.

He watched the wheel for a further few days until he felt confident enough to put it into practice. Then, he returned to the tables and on the evening of July 7, 1875 he placed his first bet, then another, and another... and won a considerable amount of money. The first day's foray against the casino netted him roughly $70,000. By the fourth day his winnings topped $300,000.

The casino officials were alarmed and highly suspicious about Jagger's success and security guards were ordered to keep him under close observation. Jagger realised he was being watched and he ensured that he did not always win. On the second night, he played the same wheel and his winning increased even further. The casino authorities decided to take drastic action and changed the wheel but Jagger had anticipated the move and had managed to mark the winning cylinder. It took him less than an hour to identify the faulty wheel... and, again, increase his growing fortune.

After several frantic days of increasingly heavy pay outs, the casino management sent an urgent message to the roulette wheel makers in Paris. They despatched a trouble shooter who quickly identified the fault and the secret to Jagger's success and he simply replaced the wheel with a new model. But during an eight-day period, Jagger had accumulated a jackpot of over two million old francs, worth in those days, well over £400,000.

When he returned next evening, the engineer soon discovered what had happened and realised that the game was finally up. He walked away from the tables and cashed in his gambling chips. He had not broken any laws nor violated any casino ruling but he appreciated that the casino management might be less than happy with his good fortune and it was perhaps an appropriate time for him to leave.

He slipped quietly out of the casino and out of France. He returned to his native Yorkshire where he gave up his job at the weaving mill and carefully invested his winnings in a string of properties in villages around Bradford. He lived quietly, though rather comfortably, and died at home, aged 61 in 1892.

He never spoke of his windfall but rumour and speculation spread and shortly after his death, a noted song writer, Fred Gilbert, inspired by the story which was sweeping across Europe and America, wrote a song, which a music hall singer Charles Coburn, would make famous across the world...

..."As I walk along the Bois de Boulogne with an independent air,
You can hear the girls declare, "He must be a millionaire!"
You can hear them sigh and wish to die,
You can see them wink the other eye,
At the man who broke the bank at Monte Carlo...!

Dan Boylan is a retired Yorkshireman, living in Wickham, Hampshire. He has been writing articles and travel features for magazines and other publications for 25 years. "My favourite genre is short fiction, which is liberally sprinkled with intrigue and the unexpected, often with humour and a twist in the tail/tale! I create imaginative story baselines with colourful character profiles and intriguing plots," he says. Dan has been a member of various writers' groups for quarter of a century producing more than sixty short stories, dramas and rattling good yarns. "My daughter claims that I am an absolute mine of useless information," smiles Dan.

AT THE HARROGATE ROYAL PUMP ROOM

At the Harrogate Royal Pump Room – a Yorkshire story, broadcast on BBC Leeds Radio on July 14, 2020

By Neville Judson

"EXCUSE me, I was wondering, the pump room seems to be closed…" Lucinda began.

"It shuts at 9.30," replied the woman she was speaking to.

"I was hoping there might be somewhere else in town."

"There's no need to go in. You can get t' water free. You have to pay inside for it – if you're daft enough. There's a tap outside on t' wall – that un."

Lucinda smiled slightly conspiratorially. "Is it the same? It does not seem quite the thing, helping oneself without paying. They say one gets what one pays for."

"I've come here twice a week for as long as I can remember and I've never had a twinge in my joints."

"You do look full of beans."

The stranger had the wrinkled face of an elderly woman but it was a lively one that seemed misplaced: her body looked so much younger. Clearly, it was a face much exposed to the harsh northern weather. The wife of a farm labourer perhaps, Lucinda thought.

"You don't look bad yersen," the woman commented. "Why would you be wanting to tak t' waters?"

Lucinda was not used to having her often admired complexion and youthful form described as "not looking bad".

"We did not come here for the waters. My husband proposed Harrogate as a pleasant destination for our honeymoon…"

"Just wed? Mine was harmless enough, bless him, but that vacant. Passed on ten years since."

"We're here to go rambling in the countryside but just for today. I said it was all right for Edward to visit the Turkish baths. While he's gone, I'm curious to discover the effects of the waters."

"You might be in for some surprises."

"Though why he's so keen to be cooped up in a room full of steam with a lot of naked men he's never met, I don't know."

Lucinda looked at the tap. "I suppose one needs to bring a glass."

"Borrow this."

Lucinda tried to hide a frown as the woman held out a grubby, chipped, enamel mug. "Oh, but don't you need to use it yourself?"

"I've finished with it for now. I was ready to go home when you turned up."

Lucinda had often marvelled at the casual ways of the lower classes and wondered what it would be like not to be constrained by the mores and formalities of her own. It was a novelty for her even to have the opportunity to walk across town alone in search of the Royal Pump Room. Separated from her family, the guests at the hotel with whom she shared an equal social status, and even her new husband, she was already beginning to feel a kind of freedom.

"If you're sure… How much does one take?"

The woman half-filled the mug from the tap. The air throughout the whole town was sulphurous enough to be a little offensive but the odour that rose from the water in the mug was truly repellent.

"Down with it," said the woman.

Lucinda turned her face away from the mug to take in a deep breath and then swallowed the water as fast as she could. She handed the mug back to the woman, who peered at it and gave her a slightly surprised look before lifting a corner of her skirt and using it to wipe around the rim.

"I never shared a mug with anyone before," Lucinda said.

"I can see that," the woman said, half to herself. "Did you say you were here to go walking?"

"That's what we're supposed to be doing."

"Come on then. If your Edward – did you say? – 's having a right old time with t' lads i' t' baths let's us lasses go for a walk in Valley Gardens."

"They tell me exercise is an essential part of the Harrogate cure."

Lucinda offered her elbow to the stranger. They linked arms and walked together into the gardens.

THE BEACH HUT

By Neville Judson

GEORGE was down at the beach hut again. There were limitless odd job opportunities in the house. For a start, one hinge on the china cabinet was coming adrift, the tap dripped in the utility room, and the cat flap would not stay shut. But all he could think about was fixing bits and pieces in the beach hut. Ever since he had bought it he had been besotted with it. He was not even coming home for lunch. He had taken a sandwich, a couple of tea bags, and the Primus stove with him.

Enid decided to fix the cat flap herself and went to get George's toolbox. When she entered the shed she discovered the petrol can in the middle of the floor. It was supposed to be the fuel for the mower. Had George filled the paraffin Primus from it?

She ran into the street without even changing out of her slippers. As she rounded the corner onto the promenade a column of flames rose halfway along the row of beach huts. When she got there, George was standing in the road and gazing at the conflagration.

"Oh, George," she said. "Thank providence you are all right."

Thank providence that sodding hut isn't, she thought.

THE END OF THE LINE

By Neville Judson

YOU have always been the gregarious type. You hate to be on your own even for an hour or two. So finding yourself alone on this station platform makes
you uncomfortable, especially at a station that hardly deserves to be called one. There is a bench halfway along the platform on the other side of the track and, on this side, a shelter that would accommodate no more than half a dozen people, with a timetable on its wall. You were expecting something better at the end of the line.

When the next train came, you thought earlier, it would stay for some minutes before it departed again. If you did not wander off too far you would hear it and have plenty of time to come back. You walked out through a gap in the rotting wooden fence and onto a deserted lane that ran beside the station. It must have been raining – the edges of the road were damp but most of its surface had dried in the cold wind. A film of desiccated mud coloured the road reddish-brown, complementing the pallid winter grass along the verges.

You saw no houses – not even in the distance. You looked back in the hope that there might be some that way, beyond the station, but there were none. All around, across the barren, brown countryside there was no sign of human presence. No buildings, no telephone lines, no electricity pylons, nothing. After walking on for a few minutes, with the wind in your face, you came upon a gate into a birch wood beside the lane. You lifted the latch and went through.

A narrow path threaded between the silver-grey stems, most of them too thin and weak to be described as trunks. Not a vestige of a leaf clung to the twigs and branches. A few hundred metres into the wood you found a little pond. You stopped and stared into the tea-brown water. There were no fish. Nothing moved beneath the surface and the water was perfectly still. No insects skated on it or hovered over it. You heard no sounds – no distant traffic or planes, no barking dogs, no birdsong, no bees. There was not the faintest rustle of twigs or grass. The wind was blowing too steadily to set them oscillating.

The path led round the perimeter of the pond and you followed it. The soft soil deadened your footsteps and they did not break the silence. You thought you saw a movement at ground level among the distant trees. A rabbit, perhaps? But it was only your imagination – something created by your eye or your mind in an effort to bring a hint of life into the scene. As you completed the circuit of the pond you stopped and listened again. You could not even hear your own breathing or heartbeat.

Why did your progress along the path draw out no earthy smell? In a damp, birch forest, why were there no smells of fungi? The sky was that drab grey-brown that portends the approach of snow. Why was there no taste of snow in the air? You were cold but it was an inner cold – more an inner hopelessness. Your hands and feet, your bare head, felt nothing – neither cold nor warmth. Looking at the lifeless grass and trees, the bare earth of the path, the pond, the sky, all of them brown or grey, you felt as though you inhabited an old, sepia picture. With a shudder, you started walking again, along the path, into the lane, and towards the station.

The steady, cold wind was in your face. You had thought it was in your face when you went the other way. You turned round. The wind was still in your face. You turned this way and that. It did not matter. Whichever way you stood, you felt the same chilling stream of air in your eyes and against your cheeks. That was when you quickened your pace and hurried back.

Now, as you stand on the platform, it occurs to you that although you have been hoping a train will come you do not know when one is due, or even if there will be another one today. What if the one you arrived on was the last and you had to face a night here by yourself? You go over to the timetable. It is not like any you have seen before. Under Arrivals there is only one entry –

3.58 p.m. The time is marked with an asterisk. You refer to the bottom of the sheet, expecting it to read Monday to Friday except bank holidays, or something like that. Instead there is just a date – February 17. That is the date today. You must get away. You look eagerly at the timetable. There is a heading Departures but there are no entries under it. You ask yourself why you chose to come to this dismal place and realise you do not know – you do not remember anything before you got on the train. The journey – you do remember that. You had been the only passenger. The only person on the train – you had not even been visited by a ticket collector. Confused memories start to come back and with them feelings of regret, of lost opportunities, of gloom such as you have never known before.

There is so much you did not do in your life; so much you should have done. There is so much you did in your life; so much you should not have done.

Standing on the platform behind the buffers you look along the line. In the distance it fades away. Not the shrinkage of perspective. Not the obscurity of mist or haze. It just fades.

You had expected something better at the end of the line.

THE LITTLE PONDERING PREACHATHON

By Neville Judson

FRED Chaucer's knees were not what they had been. He stepped awkwardly onto the upturned beer crate placed in the midst of a crowd on the village green. The parish preachathon had become an annual event in Little Pondering after the celebrated occasion when the local Baptist Minister had challenged the vicar to a war of words and they had both been defeated by the
landlord of the Cat and Bucket. Little Pondering only just had claim to be a village with its population of one hundred and fifty – one hundred and fifty one if you included the gnome in Fred's front garden – but it did have a church, a pub, and a village store that still limped along. And it had its upturned beer crate.

When it came to the preachathon, Little Pondering punched above its weight, as the chairman of the parish council had ventured to cliché during the opening ceremony. Outsiders filled the green and crowded the streets leading into it. Somebody from the local TV station was there to record the best moments (although, when the news programmes went out, the opinions of the TV station editor and the villagers usually differed on what constituted the best moments).

It was Fred's turn. "I um, ... oops!" he began, as someone kicked his beer crate to liven things up and made it wobble. "My chosen subject is Misuse of the Allotments. Stop it!" The man was wobbling his crate again. The TV camera started to roll.

"Time was, it was a privilege to get your hands on an allotment."

"Or your feet," a member of the crowd added.

Fred was not going to be flustered this early in his speech. He continued as if uninterrupted. "You were pleased to be able to get your teeth into growing food." There were chuckles from the crowd, which puzzled him, and somebody wobbled his crate again.

"It's the intended purpose of allotments – growing family sustenance. Just because we went through a few years when they were less popular, that's no reason to lower standards. There's a waiting list now, again and people should be expected to make proper use of them. I said at the time, 'No good will come of this free for all. People doing any manner of things with their allotments. The Good Lord gave us the miracles of horticulture and it's up to us to put them to best use.' That's what I said." He paused to allow the crowd to appreciate the gravity of the matter. He had read great orators were supposed to do that and he needed a moment to remember the careful wording he had planned for the next part of his speech.

The crowd stirred slightly but that was because a child sitting on someone's shoulders was waving a carrot in the air with a big bite taken out of it. An image of lush green palmate leaves comprising half a dozen or more pointed, serrated leaflets floated above Fred's thoughts as he continued. "Allotments is no place to be growing all kinds of fanciful things that are no use to man nor beast. For a start, if you want to see flowers there, what's wrong with peas and beans – runner beans – they've got lovely scarlet flowers and there's nothing better on a plate of Sunday dinner than beans picked fresh that morning. There's nothing worse than them stringy things from the supermarket.

"Anyway, as I was saying. What we need is clear rules firmly enforced."

Those sprays of rich green leaves still hovered somewhere near the bounds of his consciousness. "Healthy vegetables and nothing else. No questionable cultivations. We don't want plots used for improper purposes."

Some members of the listening crowd remembered a rumour that had gone round the village and began to guess at the herbaceous phantom that floated before Fred's eyes; others, with memories of late summer evenings on the allotments in the halcyon days when the ground was forever soft and warm, pictured youths and lasses exploring pleasures they were not supposed to know about at their age.

"There's no harm in growing a few herbs I suppose," said Fred. He was treading dangerous ground, touching on herbs. "A bit of thyme, but we don't want stuff like lavender, and we certainly don't want anything that's got nothing to do with healthy living."

His own nephew and on his own allotment. Growing that! And him the retired village policeman. Think what the consequences could have been. He had not even known what it was. Such healthy looking plants, they were. It was a shame they did not have a respectable use. He had not been able to find them in any of his gardening books. He thought he knew every weed that grew but not this one. He only realised their villainous identity when he was looking through a bunch of leaflets from the police station in town. He had gone straight home, uprooted every last plant, and piled them onto a bonfire. As he stood over the smouldering embers, strange and happy fantasies had gambolled through his reeling mind. He had a few things to say to his nephew after that.

"What about weed?" A heckler shouted from the crowd.

"Weeds! Everybody knows the rules about weeds." Fred replied. "If you don't keep your plot clear, you lose it."

"Not weeds. Weed."

There was some laughter and everybody began

to chant. "Weed! Weed! Weed!"

It was getting too much. Fred got down from the beer crate.

The man who had heckled him jumped onto it, held up his hands for silence, and addressed the crowd. "Ok, guys, calm down." He gave a sudden, mischievous grin.

"Three cheers for an excellent speech from ex PC Chaucer: Weed, weed!"

"Hurrah!"

"Weed, weed!"

"Hurrah!"

"Weed, weed, weed!"

"Hurrah! Hurrah! Hurrah!"

It was the greatest TV moment ever to come out of Little Pondering.

THE ROCK

By Neville Judson

NOTHING stirs in the grey, moonlit lane or in the pools of blackness spilling out from its uneven, dry-stone, boundary walls. There is no movement in the tracery of a lonely tree beside a gate, and the house beyond is dark and silent. Back down the lane, where it bends to the left, there is a brief, faint flicker. It comes again – stronger this time – and in a burst of light a car rounds the bend, toils past up the hill, and stops close to the gate, beneath the tree. A gust of petrol-laden air sweeps by. The engine of the car rattles to a stop. As the lights go out, the roadway – flooded red at first – is suddenly quite black until the moonlight flows back over it.

The click of a car door-catch sounds sharp and clear in the frosty air. Then another. Two men step out, two doors slam, and a key slides in and out.

A few withered fronds of bracken rustle as one man pushes between the car and the wall and walks round to the other.

"Let's walk in the moonlight for a few minutes before we go in."

Like the sounds before it the voice seems only to emphasize the silence and is quickly lost in it.

The figures come down the lane and into

the deep shadows where it curves between grassy banks. They walk on for a few minutes and then turn along a stony bridle path, hung over by stunted silver birches, blackthorn and briar. A tiny shower of ice crystals sprinkles down on the men as a solitary bird, disturbed by their passage, rises from a twig above them without a sound and flits across the moon.

Where the path leads out of the trees, a shaft of moonlight falls on the steps of a stone stile over the wall. The men stop, and then turn and climb over, dropping softly onto the springy turf. In front of them the ground rises in a close-cropped, rock-strewn mound, up to a dark rock, shaped almost like a pyramid, ten or twelve feet high. They walk diagonally to round its northern flank. From this angle it is split right through from a little to one side of its top, vertically to the ground.

The younger man goes over to the rock, places a hand against it, and then climbs easily up its sloping face, to one side of the cleft. He stops for a moment at the top and then steps across the gap of a couple of feet, walks up
the narrow ridge to the highest point, and stands gazing towards the head of the valley. Below him, his friend, leaning against the rock, turns his attention the same way.

The hills are topped with a dusting of snow and they glow white as though luminous from within. Their lower slopes – not yet touched by snow – glow more palely, with here and there a dark patch of hinted red or brown, as the moonlight refracts in the frost-covered heather and bracken. The outline of the hills is sharp against the starry sky, save for the summit of one, where a tiny wisp of cloud curls into the darkness. The man at the foot of the rock turns and reaches out to make the climb beside the crack. The stone feels cold and hard as his fingers grasp the rough holds. At the top of the slab he stops and looks across the gap towards the other figure, silhouetted against the stars. His dark hair gleams, and the graceful lines of his body stand out black against the distant milky way, or, in contrast, where the moonlight strikes, silver bright against the night sky. He shows no sign of knowing that he is watched. He does not glance towards the older man, but goes on gazing into the hills, wrapped up in his own thoughts.

His admirer holds back. He would step across the gap – climb the slope – take his friend's hand – but he senses that his approach would not be welcomed. As always, the younger man stands silent and aloof in command of his territory. And so the older man turns to look back up the valley. Below him, in the shadows deep in the cleft in the rock, a stone moves for no apparent reason and then is still.

Somewhere there is the distant rumble of an aircraft high above. His gaze wanders upwards from the hills and he starts to pick out the familiar patterns of the constellations. Silently, as he watches, a satellite begins its lonely trajectory. He follows it as it hurries across the sky, heedlessly passing between the stars, seemingly almost among them and yet never touching them, never hesitating, never turning from its course. It crosses perhaps two thirds of the distance above the valley and then, quite suddenly, as the shadow of the earth robs it of the sun's rays, it is gone.

He drops his face towards the hills again. For the first time he notices that the air is not really still: a slow, cold wind is drifting down from the snowy slopes and he feels it against his cheeks. As quietly as he came, he slips softly
down the rock face and onto the rough ground. His friend comes down after him. They walk, side by side, a little apart, their breath trailing behind them in the cool air, back along the path and up the lane to where the windows of the empty, silent house patiently watch and wait.

Neville Judson lives in rural north Yorkshire, not far from Harrogate. He grew up in south Derbyshire, where, he says, he had the good fortune to be taught by an enthusiastic and inspiring English teacher. He is well-known for his articles about caving and his scientific writing about uses of artificial intelligence in chemical research, published under the name, Philip Judson.

BOB'S JUBILEE

By Solvig Choi

BOB lay uncomfortably on his narrow metal-framed bed feeling every day of his 59 years on that dank miserable winter Jubilee morning in 1897. He pondered whether life was unfair or not as he waited for the doctor. It was true, he knew, that good people didn't often succeed in this life. You had to have power to be successful; you didn't get power by being nice. Had Bob been unsuccessful? He'd come from nothing to become head gardener at a grand house. He'd been proud of his hot house plants. Greener and lusher than anyone else's said his old mistress. Before they'd been forced to sell up to that other lot. He heard the sound of the doctor's leather-soled riding boots clopping on the stone floor.

"How are you feeling, Bob?" asked the doctor in a low voice as he approached Bob's bed in that damp and dreary dormitory in the Ripon Workhouse.

"Nowt to complain about, Doc."

Bob had, in fact, plenty to complain about. So much so that the doctor had put him on extra rations, which those in power particularly disliked as it increased taxes.

"Nice bit o' beef and brandy I get with me

meals."

The doctor continued. Bob listened without saying anything. Even the brandy wasn't enough to dent the constant nettle-sting-like pain all over his back and sides from lying down too long. He didn't want to be in the workhouse. He'd been outside every day of his life and in the garden for fifty of them, only to be unceremoniously turfed out of his cottage in a day.

We won't see a jubilee like this again in our lifetimes, thought Bob. The master and matron would be out. There'd be no one except the porter, and he might even be preoccupied with the cook.

Bob turned his head to peer over at the shrivelled old man lying in the next bed. He grimaced as he caught a bed sore. John and Norman on the other side would be the main obstacles. They hated everyone and everything. Miserable old men but they'd need to be included or they'd be sure to rat on him. They'd better take Thomas, too. Bob was thinking about what to say when Thomas spoke up.

"What did the doctor say?"

"Nowt wrong with me. Fit as a fiddle." Thomas was all right thought Bob. He'd been a chapbook salesman and sang. He'd keep them entertained with a yarn or a song.

"They were arguing in the board room about whether we can have beer or not," carped Norman.

"Again? Who won this time?" asked Bob.

"That ferret-faced Mrs Smith. Thinks us

paupers don't need beer."

"Cayvil says he's going to stand us a barrel hisself," said Thomas. "A fine upstanding gent, that."

Beer wasn't enough, thought Bob. He wanted songs played on a piano and sang together after a few drinks in a bar. How was he going to manage it? They waited around the corner from the porter's office. They had found clothes in the stores and changed out of their workhouse uniforms. Bob's wool shirt itched horribly, but he was getting out. The porter was still there. The plan about him being off with the cook hadn't panned out. They needed a distraction. It hadn't been too difficult to convince his fellow dorm mates to escape on such a special evening.

"How about Thomas tells him the cook wants to see him?" said Norman.

"That won't work. As soon as cook says she said nothing, he'll know Thomas were involved," said Burt.

"We could start a fire?" suggested Thomas.

"A bit drastic?" said Bob. He racked his brains. No one else was going to come up with something sensible.

Ten minutes later they were walking out of the workhouse gates on the way to the pub. Bob bore the pain of his gouty feet and walked almost with a spring in his step.

"That were brilliant Bob," said Thomas.

"Yeh, Bob. How did you think of that?" asked

John.

"Leaving a tap on and letting the water overflow. Genius," added Norman.

The porter would be gone for at least ten minutes. Getting back in was another question. But Bob wasn't concerned about that. The doctor had said there was nothing he could do. Bob imagined the cancer rotting his insides like the fungal blight that used to destroy his potatoes. He made himself think about the gin waiting for him.

The group heard shouting and singing and smelled the sweet hops and smoke from the nearest pub before they arrived. It was packed. Nobody would notice them. They went in and found the last empty seats. Bob asked everyone what they wanted and went to the bar. Thomas came with him.

"You're not all right, are you?"

"What are you talking about? I said I'm fine."

"We can tell by your face that it were bad news this morning."

"Let's not spoil tonight. Have you thought about how you're going to get back in?"

"I'm sure something'll come up. Maybe we can start a fire."

"Don't do that. Bung a tramp a few bob to make a commotion by vagrants block. The porter will come out to see what's happening. You can sneak in then."

"You?"

It was not like Thomas to be sharp. "We, of

course. I meant we."

Thomas was unconvinced but he stayed silent and helped to carry the drinks back to their table before going to the piano. He started with a song he must have heard on the road. It was a rowdy one about a poisoner who'd been hanged. They all joined in with the singing and merriment. They even toasted the Queen. Bob listened. He took a long swig of his gin. He relaxed into his chair and closed his eyes and sang with everyone else. A good day's work. And he wasn't going to die in the workhouse.

Solvig Choi is a wife, a mother and a soon-to-be PhD student studying museum collections outside in and inside out. She is fluent in Chinese and French and has worked in several fields, most recently volunteering at a Workhouse Museum. She is learning the violin with her daughter and enjoys yoga, photography, and playing board games online. In addition to writing, she also designs narrative videogames in twine.

CLARA & AGATHA'S

By TA Saunders

STUART Sowerby was at the pinnacle of his career. Cooking for royalty and celebrities. They would now ask for him by name. Which was why he hadn't had any time off for as long as he could remember. He was head chef at Sidney's, half way between Oxford and London. It was located within a magnificent five-storey Cotswold stone Georgian townhouse complete with sash windows and impressive front door that had just received a tasteful lick of light olive paint. Tucked away down a side street it relied on its reputation and occasional advertising in upmarket publications. Stuart's fantastic cuisine was the talk of the town. Restaurant critics had started visiting, too.

Naturally, the owner Peter Atkinson was a happy man. The restaurant was often fully booked. He kept Stuart sweet by awarding regular pay rises. But Stuart's job was having an impact on his wife and children, who never saw him.

"Where's daddy?" they would ask their bedraggled mother, Isadora. She had met Stuart in Bulgaria 15 years earlier. It had been a holiday romance that had blossomed. They had fallen madly in love, were married and soon after Clara and then Agatha arrived. It was blissful paradise. Stuart needed to be the breadwinner while Izzy was happy and satisfied being the homemaker. But neither realised the demands of parenthood. Stuart's long hours were not at all conducive to family life. He wasn't even around at weekends, which frustrated him enormously. Not only did he see very little of his family, he couldn't cook for them either. This made him very distraught, especially when he discovered that they were eating ready meals. Sadly, Izzy was not a cook. She had tried but when meals never turned out as expected she quickly lost enthusiasm. Besides the children were so demanding. There never seemed to be a minute to concentrate on anything properly. Since birth if it wasn't Agatha requiring a nappy change it was Clara wanting a feed or vice versa. And this need for attention persisted the older they got. Between them they had their poor mother wrapped around their little fingers. Stuart could feel that he was carrying more weight these days. So was Izzy, if the truth be known. It was depressing. He didn't want this life. Every day he was creating fabulous homemade dishes from scratch using the best ingredients for affluent customers, who didn't really appreciate the effort that had gone into it, as his own family would. No, the time had come for change.

The only way forward was to go it alone and run his own restaurant, he decided. This thought, dangling like a carrot, excited but also terrified him. They only rented their home at the moment, which made life easier should they need to buy a business. A move would certainly mean upheaval but then his daughters were young enough to adapt, he hoped. His dad had passed away and left Stuart some money. He was also earning a pretty good wage. But property prices down south were ridiculously high. It had always been cheaper up north but even that was expensive. Undeterred, during a late night browse of the web he had come across a run down restaurant with rooms above, near Barnsley that he could just about afford. An online viewing with Izzy saw the couple put in an offer, which was duly accepted. It all happened so quickly after that. Stuart informed his boss of his impending departure, which Peter took badly, trying to increase his salary still further to retain him.

Mortgage arranged, survey completed, six weeks later the family moved. There was much work to do but it was truly invigorating. They were all thrilled at the prospect of the new business and what it could mean for the family, if it was successful. "What are you going to call it daddy?" asked his daughters.

"Clara & Agatha's has a certain ring, don't you think?" he smiled.

"But that means we'll have to help out. Can we?"

It was certainly a family affair from the moment they arrived. Unpacking, decorating, buying tables and chairs. Izzy was in her element creating a charming and sophisticated dining room. Within weeks it was transformed from being the embarrassment of the street to the pride of it.

Importantly, Stuart was now able to cook for his family as he had always wanted to and took great pleasure watching them eating his various creations. They adored them and they were all looking so much better for it.

When he was busy writing an advertisement for the local newspaper, announcing the grand opening, in strolled the mayor, who proceeded to book the entire restaurant for the mayoral banquet.

"It will be a great pleasure sir," Stuart beamed.

"I like to support new ventures," replied the mayor. "And if your décor is anything to go by young man I am sure your food will be delicious."

This certainly focussed Stuart on compiling his menu. He had been busy making contacts with local producers but was still in the process of finalising arrangements. Well, he wouldn't need to book any advertisements for the foreseeable future, if they pulled this one off. Starters of spicy chicken noodle soup or sun-dried tomato frittata, mains of beef Wellington or vegetable hotpot and desserts of chocolate cake or fruit salad ought to make for happy customers, even if they were vegetarian, he pondered. Many Yorkshire producers wanted a place on the wine list, too. Izzy and the girls became the waitresses for this grand occasion and despite the odd broken glass and cracked plate, it was a stunning success. The profit generated that night meant that they didn't need to open for the rest of the week, which was just as well because they were exhausted.

Word spread and Clara & Agatha's soon became the place to be seen, where business people networked and slowly but surely notable locals started to dine there, too.

TA Saunders was born in Wakefield in April 1978 as it snowed. His first illustrated story titled The Tree Men was written when he was eight and he soon received his first rejection letter. A collection of his short stories simply called A Book of Short Stories is widely available.

DURHAM

FOREWORD

I wasn't born in County Durham, I'm a transplanted southerner who came to Weardale twenty-five years ago. This is my home now, I wouldn't live anywhere else. Why not? There is so much here... the finest cathedral in the country, castles, mining villages, a truly diverse and rich cultural and industrial heritage and stunning scenery. I couldn't possibly sum up this remarkable corner of North East England and I'm not going to try. To borrow Bill Bryson's famous quote from Notes from a Small Island: "If you have never been to Durham, go there at once. Take my car. It's wonderful."

But, of course, it is people who really make a place special. The people of County Durham have strong roots. They may travel to distant parts of the world but they come back. They are funny, brave, intelligent people, proud of their history, and they have taught me so much about resilience and the meaning of community. They are also story-tellers, born communicators who delight in language and the rhythms and patterns of their speech. You will meet some of those story-tellers in the following pages, let them take you on a journey to our corner of the world.

Christine Powell

POETRY

DURHAM CASTLE

More suitable for moorland Durham Castle is.
High, grey and bleak.
Except in woods by the river it is hard to see how
the ages have passed.
I can feel the gaudiness of the city in the day.
Lights on the primary colour shops,
the cheap impact of morning.
But wait till dusk and the old looms larger.
In high winds racing the sky in moaning winter.
Grey light on grey stone
spreading its identity in corners.
Then you feel the old.

Geraldine Poole

Geraldine taught for 28 years, mostly in special education. Taking early retirement she went to art college in Sunderland and graduated with a degree in fine art. Since becoming a member of North Pens Writers she has written short stories and poetry and when she isn't doing that she's making sculptures from waste materials, painting in acrylics or producing textiles.

On the left handside of the above photograph is Christine Powell's house in Stanhope, probably taken in around 1910. Christine was fascinated by the woman standing proudly in the doorway and wrote the poem below in response.
Photograph: Weardale Museum Collection

HOUSE

The photograph snapped
into my mailbox like a betrayal.
That other woman, standing at the top
of the steps, by her front door,
my front door.
And my steps, a long flight
only replaced last year.
But the handrail, plain, silvered
against the weather, slightly wonky

is exactly the same
as it was in 1910.
And now she has a name,
that other woman.
Annie Gardiner, wife
to a quarry under-manager,
Annie at the top of the steps
in her best hat,
arranged just so for the photograph.
She stares proudly into the lens,
stock still, a record for posterity
of Annie's prosperity,
but she can't know
what we know, the ripples unfurling,
the threat, the tears,
the blood shed.
How long Annie, will you stand
in your best hat
at the top of the steps?

Christine Powell

Award-winning stories by Christine Powell have been published in numerous anthologies and magazines and broadcast on BBC Radio 4. She lives in the stunning North Pennines landscape of Weardale, County Durham. Christine used to teach performing arts but now she channels her energies into writing. In 2013 she set up NorthPens, a community writing group in Weardale and runs the Weardale WordFest book festival. She is a member of Vane Women Writers' Collective and short fiction is her forte.

FREDDIE WILLIAMS'S PIGEONS

Freddie Williams kept pigeons
and over the years
he won a lot of trophies winning races with them.

He knew I worked at Barnard Castle
a commute of 39 miles.

So occasionally I would take some of his pigeons
and let them go en route.

Now this was before mobile phones
so I couldn't just ring him and say,
"On their way now Freddie."

We had to synchronise watches
so they would go at a precise time
and from a precise location
always the same roundabout near Spennymoor.

Freddie could then time them on their return
and work out which ones made the grade.

Nowadays footballers throw their
toys out of the pram
if they are on the subs bench for a big game.

They should be thankful they
aren't racing pigeons.
Any that didn't make Freddie's first team
ended up in a pie.

Jamie Tucknutt

WEARDALE SAFARI

Even though air travel is easier now,
or would be if it wasn't for the queues,
I'd still rather stay put.
Who needs abroad
when you can have a safari at home?
I mean, surely the startling colours of
goldfinches, bullfinches and long-tailed tits
are a match for any macaw.
Elephant hawk moths, leopard slugs, stag beetles
our bizarre and exotic creatures.
For tropical scents
crouched gorse smells of coconut
and pineappleweed like, well I'm
sure you can guess.
Close your eyes
and you could be in the Caribbean.
As well as geographical travel, we can time travel.
Get down among the ferns and mosses
and you could be in a prehistoric forest.
Or look at a baby heron waiting to be fed
and try telling me that pterodactyls
no longer exist.

Jamie Tucknutt

HERE'S ONE I MADE
(half a billion years) earlier

Freezing rain and piercing sleet,
a wild, wind-blasted walk in Weardale.
To be expected really. Then,
under a squelching foot in a soggy sock,
a gem of a find.
A fist-sized piece of Frosterley Marble.
A snapshot of a time long, long past.
Hard to believe,
on this very spot,
500 million years ago,
we'd have been in a warm tropical ocean.
All of those insignificant little creatures,
tiny crinoids, sponges, colourful coral,
preserved forever.
Now nestled here today in the palm of my hand.
Makes you think.
Let's find some shelter, there's tea in the flask.

Jamie Tucknutt

RETURN OF THE LAPWING

Each year, right on time.
They arrive in their thousands.
Like the caravanners; here in spring
and gone by autumn.
Peewit! Their unmistakable call.
Their impossibly broad wings,
surely stolen from a much
bigger bird.
En route, adults tell youngsters,
high over seas, mountains and lochs,
of the fabulous wonderland waiting in Weardale.
They've been coming since before the railways
and even the drystone walls crisscrossed this land.
Before the lead mines and the quarries.
They've seen agriculture and many industries
rise and wane.
They're a sure sign summer's coming, and going.
They're as much a part of Weardale
as the fossil tree and the
ford.
But one year they'll come, not too long now,
and find that humans and animals,
place different value systems on the world.
Breeding grounds, feeding grounds,
no more. Instead.

Landfill.
Just bulldozers and bin bags, smells
of diesel, detritus and decay.
Father lands beside son, his once
proud crest now crestfallen.
"My son," he'll say, fighting back tears,
"I can remember when all of this was green fields.

Jamie Tucknutt

Jamie Tucknutt is 54 years old and lives in Stanhope, County Durham with his wife Judith, their dog, two cats and a turtle. He has only recently developed a thirst for writing after a lifetime of being a voracious reader. This came about when he attended a poetry writing workshop and it has continued from there. His book Poetry as Prozac has been published by Tim Saunders Publications.

REMEMBER THE MINERS

Five of the morning.
Footprints to the gates lead.
Winding gear whirs. Caged men greeted.
Winding gear whirs. Caged men descend.

In-bye.
Pick and shovel.
Tub and gallower.
Headlamps gleam.
Water soaks.
Knees ache.
Shoulders wedge.
Hewers swing.
Winding gear whirs. Tubs rise, crammed.
Winding gear whirs. Chummins descend.

Swing the pick.
Shovel the coal.
Rest and bait.
Chummins wait.
Shovel the coal.
Swing the pick.
Tubs ready.
Out-bye.
Winding gear whirs. Caged men ascend.
Winding gear whirs. Caged men descend.

Afternoon at five.
Footsteps for the gates head.
Winding gear whirs. Men trudge alleys.
Winding gear whirs. Dad. Bathe. Eat. Sleep.

Phil Hickey

TUNSTALL RESERVOIR

When first I saw the roundness
ensnaring wild beauty, I lost.
Greys and blues, flecked white,
improving your inherent comeliness,
as wind whipped and sun sparkled.
I knew then the freedom of emotions.
Pent-up inside, they flowed from me.
No hand of winter diminished love,
nor held me from standing at your side.

Phil Hickey

STANHOPE BRIDGE

One stride and you span the ages.
From beneath your curved legs flows
the waters of life.
Time's ravages mellowed the lines,
leaving character on your countenance,
belying the passing years and people
you have known.
Long ago you knew me in my youth.
Weathered now, I stand gazing on
beauty locked.

Phil Hickey

AUTUMN LIGHT
in the Bishop's Park

To see the sun playing in your red hair brings
adolescent memories of our
togetherness to the fore.
The joys and pains, those days brought forth, are
remembered now with sad loss, that our parting
in happiness, long years ago,
could not diminish your
beauty nor my love that once I thought was lost.

Phil Hickey

Phil lives in County Durham, is a member of both Wear Valley Writers and NorthPens and has a background in engineering. Science fiction and fantasy are his main writing activities, as novel, novellas, short stories and poems. A short story and a poem of his were published in The Biscuit Factory, a Wear Valley Writers anthology, and another of his short stories is soon be published in a NorthPens collection, Writing the wild.

ORDINARY PEOPLE

"I'm a good person," we say and try to carry
on our own charade of decent life, our small
allotment of the material and mundane.
Batten down the hatches and ignore the storm
that's brewing out there, heads in the sand
of our carefully constructed illusion.
Our little house of cards - not much
protection when the wind blasts!
They did the same when Hitler marched on
Austria and Stalin executed friends, the discarded
ladders on who's now broken shoulders.
He had climbed rough-shod to power. And
now we watch again as others do the same in
every corner of the globe, yes, even our own!
Dictators, terrorists, homespun politicians.
The creed does not matter - it's simply
power, nothing less nor more.
The stolen power that draws latent corruption
to the fore, once tasted, like blood to rabid dogs,
intoxicating heady draft, that negates all else
and drains what's left of common grace.
As nature abhors a vacuum so the human
heart devoid of its humanity must flood with
that dark sea, the rising tide of depravity.
Were they extraordinary men who collected
the teeth and hair of murdered Jews in the
squalor and horror of Auschwitz?

Or were the kamikaze pilots of the east a less than
human breed, evil beyond the common lot?
Were they not rather the ordinary man
down the street?The kindly father, friendly
neighbour... in fact not so different from
ourselves if we will stop to think.
It was too late by the time they saw and
had their heads forced out of sand into
storm. With bleary eyes they saw
children, begotten by themselves and yet
strangers to all they thought they held dear.
Their minds and hearts stolen by a state intent
on washing common grace and merciful
conscience from their tender souls.
Mindless army of automatons blinded and
deafened to all but their master's call
efficiently programmed to do all required,
willing to betray with careless ease even
parent, brother, sister, friend with a kiss.
And is it any different now? The human
bombs who walk our brazen streets or stalk
our virtual shrines do they not bear
the unmistakable face of our shared
humanity? Poor puppets on a string, dupes
and victims; all lambs to the slaughter.
And do we really think that we - WE?! The refugees
from truth and history! - would fare any better
at the point of a gun or Twitter bayonet?
Or believe our flabby western minds
impervious to the subtle seeping poison
of a lifetime of delicious drip-fed lies

Crafted to flatter our folly and feed our
hate as nectar in a honey trap?
The trap has sprung before we find
we have no ground or soul or fibre
left on which to make a stand.
Now is the time to cast aside our brittle vestige,
flimsy construction of ourselves; the phoney
happy spectres that we project each fleeting day
and through the ubiquitous ether seeking
affirmation from the watching world (the world-
wide web and doesn't it entangle us all so well?!)
How will we fare when shiny surface scratches
our substance bubbles out? Like a candle in the
wind, will it light our path when darkness comes?
Like a house built on sand, can it shelter or
provide a single solid foothold in the storm?
Pitiful rags of threadbare ego…how will they
warm our soul in winter's bleakness?
Then while we still have the fading
autumn light let us look hard and long
in the impartial mirror of the past
open the honest book of our human
story and see our own faces staring
back from the glass of history
we are the sheep, the foolish, stupid sheep.
And yet a mighty throng, an army, if we
will, to battle the darkling tide.
If once we would own our feet of clay we may look
up beyond the head of gold. If only we had eyes to
see and hearts to understand, while it is still day
for the night comes swiftly on when

no man can work or speak.

Jennifer Denning

THE SHORELINE
of my mind

The shoreline of my mind
is littered with the scars and shells
debris of the wars I've fought
over the boundaries of my thoughts
within myself.

My quiet thoughts are still
a hundred snowy sheep
that pasture on the balmy hill
and among the dew and clover
have their fill.

But always one or two prodigals
will break away from that contented flock
and wander off down streams and dells
where tempting wild violets bloom
and water flows.

Like the meeting of a thousand little streams
the estuary of my mind
is churned and dark with silt and dregs
of half forgotten dreams that chafe
the rawer edges of my soul.

And so on into the vast and briny deep
the wonderers have slipped the net

and got away
sailing over waves thrown up from depths
of equal light and dark.

The ever moving restless sea
of human shifting loves and fears
a boundless ocean-tide of changing hues
until at last we reach that distant shore
where silver waves are lapping gently.

Jennifer Denning

Jennifer, who lives in High Shincliffe, just outside the city of Durham, is writing a novel, which is set in Durham and Northumbria.

A SILVER THREAD

A silver thread runs through the Dale,
bisecting field and wood and shielding,
running beside old river Wear,
a permanent way on valley floor.
A silver thread runs through the Dale,
a lifeline once for hardy folk,
working the mines and upland farmsteads,
produce taken door to door.
A silver thread runs through the Dale,
silent now but once alive,
with engines steaming, trucks revealing,
marble, stone, cement and more.
A silver thread runs through the Dale,
and children play where trains once ran,
the railway, oh so proud and noble,
today is part of Dale folklore.
A silver thread runs through the Dale,
repaired, reborn a heritage line,
with engines steaming, coaches gleaming,
day trippers now instead of ore.

Mike Kane

Michael was born in 1949 in Gosforth, Northumberland and grew up in a home where the love of books was encouraged. He began writing fiction when he was eleven. In 1967 he wrote a romantic novella, which was packed away, forgotten, rediscovered during a house move and self-published as The Ghost of Christmas Past. Michael is a member of the NorthPens community writing group based in Weardale. He is happily married and lives with his wife in a remote hamlet high in the North Pennines on the border of Northumberland. They have three grown-up children and seven grandchildren.

BOUDY

Boudy is the dialect word for the little bits and pieces of broken pottery or other discarded items that people dig up while they are digging in the soil. Not valuable – just items of curiosity. The poem considers three pieces of 'boudy' and who they may have once belonged to: a piece of broken Sunday-best china, a piece of an earthenware bread bowl and a piece of a Weardale lead miner's clay pipe.

There's boudy in the garden; boudy blue and
white, lying quiet in the darkness just
waiting for the light.
Boudy in the garden; boudy brown and cream,
sleeping through the passing years,
but still able to dream
of times when it was whole and handled with
great care; a time when it was useful,
or treasured, or just there.

China teacup, willow patterned, delicate
and fine, passed on from a granny
right down the family line;
only used on Sundays or when company
came to call, until Elsie's fingers slipped
and it had a fatal fall.

"Eeh, I am that sorry!" was all that she could

say - and Hannah hid her tears, as she
swept the bits away.
Wide and deep and strong was Mary's bowl
for bread but, knead a stone of flour,
and her arms would feel like lead.
No time for rest - she's still got clothes to
scrub; so dough beside the fire to rise,
she'd go and fill the tub.

But once, in her hurry, she set it far too
near. It cracked from top to base and
her Mam - she skelped her ear.
Digging lead ore all the week, tired to the
bone - and still a tatty patch to dig
waits for him at home.

There's very little solace to lighten up his
load; a clay pipe and some baccy,
the promise of warm food.
Sarah brings him tea out, nicely hot and sweet.
He turns too quick; the snapped pipe
lies broken at his feet.

There's boudy in the garden, boudy in
the soil; each piece of it a record of
someone's life and toil.
Oh, to see the hands that held it, for that
final time; never knowing that one day
the next touch would be mine.

There's boudy in the garden and, when I dig

it up, I make a link with lives from here;
we share the broken cup.
What boudy will be left behind when I leave
this place? Will someone one day find it
and try to see my face?

Carol Madeline Graham

Carol lives in Upper Weardale, County Durham. Her first book, A Shoulder on The Hill was published in 2020 and her second book A Shoulder to Lean On will be published in October 2022. Both are gentle, humorous and sometimes poignant memoirs of her life in Weardale, the glories of the wildlife and the challenge of the seasons. Carol is a retired special needs teacher, who feels privileged to have lived in Upper Weardale for the last twenty years. Her previous books, Driving Force and Driving Finish were autobiographies of the carriage driving world.

SHORT STORY

THE WITNESS FOR THE PROSECUTION

By Mike Kane

MISS Grey sat in a corner listening. She was always listening because that was her job; to be ready at a moment's notice to obey Sir Reginald's instructions.

Sir Reginald duBious was a high-flying city financier; duBious by name and dubious by nature. He had a large portfolio of business interests; many legitimate, some – less so. He lived in one of those smart eye-wateringly expensive apartments on Canary Wharf.

Miss Grey had been on Sir Reginald's staff for three years now, long enough for Sir Reginald to hardly notice her; just as he hardly noticed the chef who prepared his gourmet meals or the maid who served them or the chauffeur who drove him in his limousine. They had become part of the furniture on the periphery of his self-important life.

Miss Grey made appointments; kept an eye on the time, switching on the lights as dusk fell; drawing the curtains; ensuring the coffee machine was switched on for meetings; waiting for any instructions and acting on them immediately; Sir

Reginald's efficient personal assistant.

Sir Reginald and his cronies were gathered around the dining table after dinner, enjoying port and cigars. The chef was finished for the day and the maid had withdrawn with the dirty plates. Only unobtrusive, super-efficient Miss Grey remained, sitting quietly in the shadows in the corner listening.

The group around the table had obviously forgotten that she was there as they started to discuss a business venture that was very non-legitimate indeed. Their voices were low as they plotted an extremely daring stock exchange swindle.

A few months later

The high-profile trial made all the headlines as well as the main news channels. People were shocked at the audacity of the city fat cats and their failed swindle. They nodded with approval at the stiff sentences handed out by the judge, deeming that justice had been done.

Miss Grey was called as a witness for the prosecution. Sir Reginald had covered his tracks well, destroying his files and wiping his computer but he had forgotten about his PA and it was her detailed evidence that sealed his fate and that of his accomplices.

However, the audacious swindle wasn't the main reason for the trial's publicity which sent a shockwave through society. It was because of Miss Grey herself. For Miss Grey wasn't human at all.

Miss Grey was a machine, installed in millions of homes and offices throughout the world; the perfect, ubiquitous PA programmed to perform tasks, control smart devices, always listening and making notes...

Michael was born in 1949 in Gosforth, Northumberland and and grew up in a home where the love of books was encouraged. He began writing fiction when he was eleven. In 1967 he wrote a romantic novella, which was packed away, forgotten, re-discovered during a house move and published as The Ghost of Christmas Past. Michael is a member of the NorthPens community writing group based in Weardale. He is happily married and lives with his wife in a remote hamlet high in the North Pennines on the border of Northumberland. They have three grown-up children and seven grandchildren.

NORTHUMBERLAND

FOREWORD

When I was growing up, my family and I would talk about the next town, village or seaside resort we would visit next, as we sat and ate the cuisine of the north. Favourites of the past were black pudding, peas pudding and always fresh fish from the local monger caught from the North Sea. The decisions made would only include the county of Northumberland where there are so many
wonderful places to see. My memories are of the smells of the sea, the hillside country farms with the cute lambs being born in the springtime and the towns where those smells linger from the market stalls full of freshly baked bread and pastries. Muscles, shrimps and cockles being eaten on the dock of my favourite seaside village whilst gazing over the wall to a view of the huge castle in the distance. Seagulls trying to steal the delicious fish and chips as we ate them out of newspaper. Long beaches to walk along or on a summer's day a dip in the ocean.

Memories of becoming a teenager often still travelling to those familiar places. Showing off my home county to friends from the city. Turning eighteen to eventually participate in the gossip with local folk from each village inn that I visited. Tasting the delicious mead originally made by the monks from Holy Island and still being brewed from the distillery on that same island.

In the autumn and winter the best time to visit Kielder Forest, a haven for wildlife and awarded a Gold Tier Dark Sky status with its observatory is great for stargazing. Pack up your binoculars, a deckchair and a hot drink and sit back to enjoy the star-studded show.

Not forgetting the friendly communities where everyone can leave a door open is still a privilege to have in Northumberland, especially during these days of uncertainty.

Peaceful views of the hills and trees with horses abound trotting about to their hearts' content, right nearby. Woods to take dogs and the bleating of sheep in the nearby fields is what I experience everyday. Being surrounded by nature is a good way to describe Northumberland.

Living in several places either in the United Kingdom or overseas has proven to me that I know where my home is. Home pulls at the heart strings and never let's go until you arrive. Being an adventurer by nature has not slowed me down just yet but having Northumberland to call home is a blessing.

And it is home to some hugely talented writers and poets, too, showcased in this beautiful book.

Joy Eckert

POETRY

HADRIAN'S WALL...
AND BEYOND!

Trees surround my woken self
some fallen due to savage storms.
A morning dew falls upon my skin as I
walk alongside our early friends.
The songs of nature fill the air within
the woodland near to sunlight.
Our voices low, listening with smiles abounds
next to fields and hills and sounds.
Sounds now of bleating lambs below the
valley so low but also so bright.
Bright with a green we have ever seen.
We walk amongst the vast wilderness
our voices louder
not the shouting of the city but calm and serene .
The farmer waves as he walks with
canny lambs just born.
Our next stop on our hike is along
ancient stones towards the ocean
in our sites we see it ahead a blue so
bright we have to squint.
The white foamy waves are such an invite
quite a saintly and heavenly attraction
bringing to us such emotion.
Turning our heads, we see a castle upon a hill
a proud specimen from days of old still

standing as the years unfold.
A cross is planted in the soil for all
to touch and pray and hope
that one day we will return to this
island of saints and mead.
What a place, what a thrill
taking our time to enjoy the view then
off again our sprightly few.
Our next stop is a castle of distinction
where Harry Potter is known in fiction
children from around the globe with
wands and gowns faces aglow
so different from long ago when dukes
and formalities were on show.
These moments of watching all of
this splendour are taken
as we move towards the town to
belong to the many
our faces alight at the market
stalls, our senses awaken
scoffing on our moreish treats we turn
to move towards our waiting bus.
Northumberland is waiting for
young and old to explore
sampling the stotties, kippers and local ale
you'll certainly find you'll only want more.

Joy Eckert

NORTH EAST BOUND
(earplugs not included)

Excited children sharing toys
parents under pressure
put that down, pick that up
chant goes on, sleep takes over.
Quiet reigns, no more noise.
Grumbling bellies, stopping a must
hurried feet leave, now alone.
Fingers move on mobile, friend I trust
plants need watering "key under stone".
Fed, watered ready to go
kids put on a show.
Nearing destination it's worth the woes
buckets and spades dipping our toes
seagulls in flight, enormous castle to the right
Northumberland ... county to boast its
saintly culture and heavenly coast.

Joy Eckert

Joy Eckert is author of *In Memory Of...* and *Higher Love*. "I just love to write," she says. "It's my saviour in life." This is her first poem. Joy lived in Northumberland all of her childhood until she met her American husband in Spain. She moved to

Germany for a year then on to America where she lived for fifteen years and had a daughter. Moving back to the UK in 2001 they became involved in the hospitality business. She moved to Great Malvern, then Stratford-upon-Avon before returning to Northumberland in 2018. Joy lives in a small hamlet with her husband Tim and their dog Rose.

LINDISFARNE

I met myself on the island
when the moon held back the sea
and the dunes swathed in mist
whispered the old stories
of church bones cradled close
to the well where Jenny fell
of fossil beads and honey mead
and a man who talked to crows.
As I walked to welcome my familiar
sand crunched beneath my toes.
We dropped a stone in water
And made a perfect O.

M Elaine Murphy

M Elaine Murphy has lived in Northumberland for the last thirty years. Holy Island has a special place in her heart. "I can still remember driving across the sand in my dad's battered old Morris in the days before the causeway," recalls M Elaine, who is originally from Tyneside. "I think the island is a place where you can catch up with yourself. Maybe there's something in the ancient rhythm - it's very soothing. I also like the idea that the island is both in time and out of time.

TANK TRAPS, ALNMOUTH

tank traps
sunken with age
into the bleached sands
a few have lost the battle and disappeared
and break up the lines
of silent concrete defenders
they wait
against an enemy that never came
but the enemy that conquered them was time
that tipped them sideways
and absorbed them into the landscape of azure sea
clear ebbing tide
and miniature footprints in the sand

Helena Hinn

Helena Hinn lives in Newcastle upon Tyne and has been writing poetry since the 1980s. She has been published widely including in Oxford University Press and Faber & Faber anthologies.

COBDEN BURN CLEUGH

this crisp lightingness
clear cuts through autumn's
breeze into the leafyness
and such illumination of
colourings feasts the eye
beyond any this northern lights
could pretend, as pretending
that was and never did
hints at what natural
beautyness is caught this
day by Cobden Burn cleugh.

Mark Carr

DUSK AT CHEVIOT HILLS

too many smells in the wind brushed hillside dusk
as honey heather hovers down
rumbling cleugh cliffs
to fern-fresh forever spores firing
air-bound eastwards
while underfoot moss-beds move
green paved as paths.
such dusty haze calls in the night
of these cheviot curves, cold crisp silhouetting
by this evening glow-ball burns
deep down beyond
and silence echoes peace far further than quiet.

Mark Carr

ON HANGMAN'S HILL

on hangman's hill
I sat
as
hornets hummed
I tipped
my hat
to those
who dangled
and died
to them that
shot
and cried
so whispered souls
across and down
to devil's water
by
rowen-tree cleugh
then sadness
caught me
to think
and that,
that too much blood
was
spilt and spat.

Mark Carr

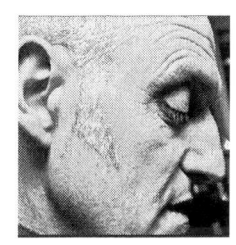

Principally Mark is an artist. He has been making and exhibiting art in the UK and abroad since his teenage years, gaining a BA(Hons) Fine Art in 1984, a PGCE in 1992, and an MA Fine Art in 1994. However, writing has always been a large part of his creative output, with poetry being a great calling in his life. He has travelled widely across Europe, North America, India and Australasia. Mark was born and educated in the north east of England where he now lives and works.

SHORT STORIES

SANCTUARY

By Gwenda Major

HE flexes his cramped fingers. With his right hand he kneads his temples, squeezing his eyes shut for a grateful second. Yellow serpents dance behind his closed lids. It is summer but the sky is dull, the light seeping cautiously through the narrow window. His eyes suffer. It is to be expected.

Four hours have passed since matins. His stomach stirs at the thought of food. Since the famine the rations have become meagre but saliva still fills his mouth as he imagines the thin porridge and the coarse bread.

A throb of toothache makes him wince. His whole jaw aches. When this work is done he must find time to go to the infirmary. The tooth will have to be pulled.

He picks up the goose feather quill once more, dips the nib into the pot of sluggish brown ink and braces his arm on the bench to allow him to hold the broad nib parallel to the guidelines. He stoops over the page and carefully traces the final words of the text 'eratque cum bestiis, et angeli ministrabant illi' (and the angels administered to him). The lampblack letters appear one by one, evenly and smoothly, released by the rhythmic flow of his quill. The ink glistens wet.

Anticipation stirs in him like a waking bird. He straightens his crooked back and absently scratches his neck where the rough wool of his casula has rubbed a sore place. He picks up the tablet from the bench and examines the intricate design traced in the shallow layer of wax. Strange serpentine birds, the island's Cormorants, twist along the uprights of the letter M, their bodies twining with interlaced ribbons of colour.

His assistant interrupts him with the tray of pigments, bright pools of colour coddled in their eggshell hollows. The lad places them carefully on the bench, relieved to have delivered his precious burden intact.

"How goes the next batch of vellum?"

"They will take it off the stretching frames tomorrow", the lad says, adding proudly, "I am preparing the paste of lime with flour, egg white and milk for rubbing in."

"Then I trust your paste will make the vellum perfectly smooth this time. The last batch still had some hairs on it."

An unbidden image of smooth white flesh rises to the surface of his mind. The swell of a woman's breast, the curve of a thigh. He sighs. He will need to confess these thoughts at compline tonight. The devil creeps in wherever he can. He waves the lad away, keen to return to his great task.

For the spaces between the arcades of the letter M he has sketched a contorted, sinister beast with the body of a snake and jaws full of predatory teeth. The image came to him after the dreadful portents earlier in the year. He still wakes sweating in the night remembering the whirlwinds, the blinding flashes of lightning and the fiery dragons that flew through the air, making the brothers scatter to their huts where they cowered in terror. Then the famine struck so all knew it had been an omen. Now their stocks of food are low and the winter is still far off. At least they are safe here on this holy island.

He pushes away the dark thoughts impatiently and takes a deep breath to steady himself. Meticulously he begins to transfer the design from the tablet to the vellum. The sinews of his hand are taut as he grips the stylus. There can be no errors.

Later the bell rings for terce. He covers the eggshells with a cloth and unfolds himself slowly. His muscles protest, cramped from the morning's work yet he can hardly bear to leave the manuscript.

The chants of the terce mass break into colours in his head – red and indigo, blue and yellow. The words of the readings swirl in intricate spirals, drifting up to heaven. Then the relief of dinner is profound, the bread and cured pork disappearing all too soon, washed down with watered beer. He squats to go to the toilet before returning to his hut to lie down for a siesta. He must rest and attend the service of none prayers before he can devote himself again to his task.

At last he takes up the goat-hair brush and dips the tip into the yellow ochre paint. His hand wavers at first but he masters it and little by little follows the first vertical of the letter, filling in a tiny channel with the bright pigment. His heart soars and dips with his brush. This is his ecstasy. Nothing else exists now, only the tiny movement of his brush. He applies a little kermes red to the undulating birds in the verticals. Then he wipes the brush on a rag and dips it into the shell of turnsole purple and begins to work on the twisted contortions of the beast. Under his hand it comes to life, its snarling head, its staring eye, its fearsome fangs. With great care he applies an infinitesimally small amount of precious lapis lazuli to the eye of the creature.

Finally he allows himself to sit upright. The initial is alive with colour now, the birds and the snarling beast penned within its verticals.

A shout. Then another. It is still daylight, another hour or more before supper. He eases himself off his stool and steps to the door of the hut. A brother monk runs past gesticulating wildly. He leaves the sanctuary of his cell and walks a few paces forward. A bell has started to ring. Not the calm rhythm of the vespers bell but a wild frantic warning that strikes fear into his heart. Several brothers are standing nearer the shoreline. He follows the line of their outstretched arms with his eyes. The sky is streaked with lurid light. To his horror he sees dragon heads rising and falling on the horizon. It is coming.

Award winning author Gwenda Major was brought up in the north east. Her passions are for genealogy, gardening and graveyards. Her stories have featured in numerous print and digital publications such as the Fiction Factory, Retreat West, Brilliant Flash Fiction, Write-Time and Cranked Anvil. Several stories have also been broadcast on local radio. Her most recent success was winning the Crossing the Tees short story competition in 2022. Gwenda has written four novels and three novellas. Her novella, Offcomers won first prize in an Open Novella Competition in 2016.

FREEDOM FROM SHAME

By Joy Eckert

THE sun is reflecting off the water in the small puddle from last night's rain as I sit in the peacefulness of my colourful garden. It is showing off the doomed insects that had faith in the liquid, giving them solace. Instead, they succumbed to their doom. Their ignorance certainly didn't become bliss.

Not long ago my life became very similar in the way that I was ignorant in the true meaning of the word. I was savagely raped as I walked home from my shift at work. I was a waitress in a nice restaurant where supposedly nice people dined. I was so wrong.

The night it happened had been a good night. Parties of tipsy diners who were celebrating birthdays or graduations were keen on leaving huge tips. I was happy to put almost one hundred pounds in my bag that night, which was from a share between three of us. After the usual banter with colleagues before my walk home, I noticed a regular coming from the area of the bar, who had asked me out a couple of times over the past few weeks. He seemed very nice, quite respectable and nicely dressed in his smart jeans, white open neck shirt and, "I really like your trainers," I had told him one evening.

I wasn't interested in going out with him as I was still getting over my last break up with a man who I thought was the one. I was quite happy with the other stuff in my life as I was renting a nice apartment not far from the city where I worked, which was only a ten-minute walk away. It was a Victorian terraced building in a small quiet street with trees to look out on when I sat at my table at the window. I loved the huge shiny black front door with its antique door knocker. My friend Alice came over to spend the night when she could, which was almost every other weekend now that she had changed jobs. No more weekends working ever again was her motto.

But that night in September my life was about to change. I noticed that nice man coming up behind me as I walked towards my home. I heard him shout, "Hey Lyndsey."

I turned my head to watch him heading towards me. Not thinking he would harm me I waited until he was by my side. He grabbed my elbow and said, "Thought I would never catch up with you," trying to catch his breath then, "Fancy a night cap somewhere?"

"No not tonight em..."

"Jack...it's Jack. Remember that night I watched you in that night club a few weeks ago? You were all over me with your "Jack look how I move."

I nodded and apologised and told him that I

won't forget it again. The night he is talking about was in a club that Alice and I liked to go to dance. He was there with a mate and I was a bit drunk. Alice tried to control me but I already knew that he fancied the pants off me so I flirted with him and egged him on. I thought he was quite hot at the time. Obviously, he liked to be the one that took charge of the flirting so he only just watched as I danced near to him showing off my sexual moves.

In the next few minutes after apologising and thankfully getting nearer to home he dragged me into the nearby bushes then pushed my face down in the soil so I couldn't scream.

"Now I can be in charge of you," he said as he forced his way inside me. "You won't forget my name now will you Lyndsey?"

I was pushed around on the ground so much that it felt like my eye lids would bleed. I felt ashamed lying there when he finally left me to struggle back up. But before he left me there to rot, he quite happily urinated on me. The warm liquid flowing down my back made me feel even more nauseous. I must have laid there another fifteen minutes or so before I could manage to stand after my ordeal. My whole body felt as if it was torn in two. I struggled my way out of the smelly surroundings then realised that my rapist must have taken my mobile phone or it had fallen out of my bag as I searched for it with my still grubby, soiled hands but with no luck. I carefully staggered home whilst crying so hard my vision was blurred.

When I eventually got myself indoors, I dug out an old phone, fired it up and called Alice. Within half an hour she helped me to get in the bath while carefully washing my hair and my disgraceful body.

"It's my own fault," I told her. "I shouldn't have egged him on that night. You saw how I looked at him. My eyes were seducing him." I cried so hard into her face.

"Don't be so stupid, Lyndsey. It's not your fault. He raped you. He should be jailed for what he has done to you."

I enjoyed the comfort Alice gave me with her gentle hands carefully washing away the dirt and grime that he forced on to me. Alice called the police the next morning. I wouldn't let her that night as I felt ashamed.

I sit here in my peaceful garden almost one year to the day that I was savagely raped and wait for the company of Jane my therapist. She has helped me to find freedom again from that terrible night. I became reclusive and blamed myself for his behaviour. Alice had told me that it wasn't wrong to admire his trainers or dance beside him. I now know with thanks to the help I am getting that I will find peace and hope in my heart again.

NORTHUMBERLAND ROAD

By Joy Eckert

Then

AS I settled down for the evening, hands wrapped around my mug of coffee and feet tucked under my legs, I reflected upon the past few hours. Nick upstairs reading the girls a bedtime story to take their minds off the last few hours before we returned home.

The smell and the screams of everyone running for safety. We couldn't quite believe what was happening right before our eyes.

Our day out was supposed to be one of excitement. But that had been put to a stop when the unexpected disaster came out of nowhere. I'd noticed an elderly man stepping out of Josies café stopping as he tried to place his checked cap on top of his balding head. Then suddenly, "Fire in the window," he shouted - finger pointing towards the flames. His voice growing in strength as the situation became dire. His cap now underfoot.

We immediately turned our heads to see sparks flying from a large spotlight shining on a brightly coloured display in Carrington's, then the noise came. BANG! The window blew out and crashed onto the pavement. The screams were deafening. Nick and I grabbed our girls and ran as fast as our legs could move while each carrying a child. When we were safely enough away, we placed our children on the ground looking back to see the fire coming out of the roof of Carrington's. A unique department store, which has served the community forever seemingly. The sound of the fire engines was a relief but those frightening banging sounds continued. I held away my tears so as not to upset the girls even more. They achieved that quite easily as we stood watching the horrible event from a distance. I wiped their noses as they asked where Santa would go now. I looked at Nick, lost for

words. He took over by telling them that Santa would always find them no matter what happened.

Carrington's was well known for its Christmas window and Santa Claus. Every year we would happily show up to gaze in amazement. Taking photos of our children when it was their turn to tell Santa their hearts' desire. Afterwards each child's face lighting up with excitement carefully choosing a secret brightly wrapped gift out of the special Christmas box.

Northumberland Road was a place where families get together to enjoy the ambience of such a traditional area, which is over one hundred years old. The market place with the sounds of folk bartering to get the best deal. The quaint shops standing side by side showing off their goods on display out in the open to attract customers. And our special place, Mr Solley's Homemade Sarsaparilla Shop. The memories of my sister and I excited as dad took us for the first time and then after we couldn't get enough of the delicious drink. Continuing the tradition with my children hoping they would love it just as much as I did is a great success. Twirling round on the newly fitted red leather and chrome bar stools as the girls wait for the liquid treat and chatting with Mr Solly Junior as I stare out of the bay window thinking about my late dad as we strolled down this old cobbled street. Those cobbles have partially been replaced with paving stones but the character is still in abundance. Thankfully before the fire, our first stop was pushing that jingling door into those magical sweet smells. Swigging down the taste of memories from the past.

But that had suddenly disappeared from our lives as the fire spread very quickly throughout the area leaving a few with only smoke damage according to the local rag. The following day Nick and I were still in shock as we trudged through our work days with the news of the tragic event at Northumberland Road being mentioned from everyone's lips. People of all ages tried to come to terms with the fact that returning would be a long way off. With sadness in our hearts, we told our girls that Solly's would also be one of the shops that would be out of action for a while. Tears on the verge of tumbling down onto their flushed cheeks, our conversation quickly turned to what would replace our weekly run into town.

We decided the best thing to do would be to write down some ideas. Olivia, our eldest wanted to write a letter to Mr Solly to tell him that he would be missed so very badly. Sarah on hearing that put up her hand like in school to ask if she could have help with writing a letter to Santa to tell him and his reindeer about the closing of Carrington's. "That's a wonderful idea," I said, cheering up.

"But Mummy I hope he really knows where to go to find us?"

Nick piped in reminding them that Santa just knows. They both accepted his explanation and settled down, carefully concentrating on their task at hand.

Now

I awake at the sound of our daily newspaper falling onto our welcome mat. As I descend our staircase then bending down for the paper, I wander into the kitchen seeing Nick sitting with coffee in hand.

"Hey, what's up? You still look tired love."

"I'm ok." I sit and unfold the news as he passes my first caffeine shot of the day.

"Oh my God, Nicholas," I say in amazement.

"Oh my God, what Eleanor?" he replies with a

smirk.

"Look at the headlines." I throw the paper in his direction whilst popping bread into the toaster.

"Great news Elle. After all this time."

I kiss his cheek. "Can't believe it, after eight years of planning and all the red tape."

Even though the years have been many and our girls are now teenagers, we are excited about going to the celebrations of the re-opening of Northumberland Road. First stop? ... Mr Solly's Homemade Sarsaparilla, of course.

Joy Eckert is author of *In Memory Of...* and *Higher Love*. "I just love to write," she says. "It's my saviour in life." This is her first poem. Joy lived in Northumberland all of her childhood until she met her American husband in Spain. She moved to Germany for a year then on to America where she lived for fifteen years and had a daughter. Moving back to the UK in 2001 they became involved in the hospitality business. She moved to Great Malvern, then Stratford-upon-Avon before returning to Northumberland in 2018. Joy lives in a small hamlet with her husband Tim and their dog Rose.